The Prince's Spy
a story of Egypt

by Hilary Cawston

Published by Chiavari

Other titles by Hilary Cawston

Seeking Osiris (2014)

The year is 1225 BC.

The place is Mennefer, ancient capital city of Kemet.

Ramesses II is celebrating his fifty-fifth year as King.

His son, the Crown Prince Khaemwase has decided to die.

Enter Sunero, agent to the Royal Heir, the Prince's Spy.

Chapter One

Sunero closed the door gently behind him and walked with droop-ing shoulders to the dais against the far wall. The man sitting on the edge of the platform held out a cup, which Sunero took without a word. He sat down beside his friend and after taking a long swallow of the sharp-tasting wine, he sighed, 'He's dying.'

'He's been ill before,' his companion said.

'Not like this. It's as if the heart has gone out of him. He doesn't care any more. There's nothing left to do, nothing left to discover, nothing to look forward to.'

'What do the doctors say?'

'What do they know? There's nothing obviously wrong with him, no fever, no pain. He's simply given up.'

'That's ridiculous. We can't just let him go.'

'Perhaps we have to. Perhaps that's what he wants.'

Silence fell between the two men as their minds drifted, lost in their individual memories, while in the adjoining room their master the Crown Prince, Khaemwase, Heir to the Thrones of the Two Lands, lay enmeshed in his own thoughts. Life had been long and, on the whole, enjoyable. He had outlived three older brothers to become his father's heir but the King had outlived everyone. There was little prospect now of Khaemwase ever wearing the Double Crown. The King was indestructible. Not that the Prince had truly relished the idea of kingship. He had had more freedom, more experience of real life, as a younger son. He had made friends who had respected him for what he was rather than for what he might become. He had never tolerated fools or hangers-on, nor had he tried to make himself popular. People must take him as they found him, and few found him to be an easy man. But those who had come close to him had stayed and were, to a man, loyal. Like Sunero.

A sharp-witted, nimble-fingered man with an eye for detail, which had served Khaemwase well on many occasions, Sunero's talents had been recognised when he was a lowly clerk in the Prince's estate office. Khaem-wase had quickly promoted him until at the age of twenty Sunero became the supervisor of the Prince's valuable holdings around the Great Lake. While the face he showed to the world was that of an able and efficient land agent, Sunero's particular skills were frequently required in other areas, which often had little to do with estate management. He was Khaemwase's Eyes and Ears or, as he was more commonly known, the Prince's Spy.

Sunero had done all those things Khaemwase had wished he could have done for himself. If he had been born into a humbler family, Khaemwase could have enjoyed those challenges and adventures, those dangers from which a prince of the royal house was necessarily protected. Nevertheless, he had lived a full life with perhaps more than a prince's share of excitement and his experience had been enriched by Sunero's reports. The Prince's Spy had given his master access to people and places beyond the knowledge or caring of most princes. Sunero had a knack for uncovering highly amusing and often mentally stimulating human problems, which he brought to Khaemwase for his attention and entertainment. Sunero had given the Prince some of his most satisfying intellectual moments, had kept him amused throughout the most boring of times. Khaemwase's life had been made complete by these interludes – almost. There was just one thing, such a little thing, or maybe it was not so little, just one thing that he needed to know before he could die content. He wanted Sunero to volunteer the information, for a Prince should not have to beg favours from his servants. And yet he was not sure that Sunero knew all the facts of the matter. Perhaps he would never know and that would be his greatest regret. He was annoyed by the existence of this gap in his knowledge, he who had spent a lifetime in study, who was recognised as Egypt's most educated man. His education was incomplete because there was still some-thing that he did not know.

Sunero dragged his wandering mind back from uncomfortable recollection, drained his cup and said to his friend, 'He ought to be told. Now, before it's too late. It's not fair to keep him in the dark, not after all this time.'

'The story has waited this long wthout being told, a little longer won't hurt,' the other man snorted.

Sunero could not tell whether it was with contempt or laughter. He turned sharply to look straight into those bright, quartz-hard eyes. 'Whatever you think of him, remember what he did for you. The past is gone, all debts have been paid. Would it hurt to tell him? He deserves to know.'

The younger man snapped back, 'What you mean is, you want to know. It's been eating at you for years. You can't bear to have a case unfinished. You want to close the file.'

Sunero would not be goaded. 'It's his file,' he said, 'he has the right to close it himself.'

'All right then.'

Sunero was taken by surprise. His mouth fell open. This time, his companion laughed aloud. 'Yes, I mean it. It can do no harm to tell. I know you can be trusted and I've trusted him with my life before now. Fetch the file. We'll tell him a bedtime story.'

When the two men were announced, the Prince knew at once why they had come. He impatiently waved his body servants from the room and ordered them not to return until Master Sunero should summon them. He reclined on the day bed, his heavily pleated gown gathered around him hiding his still athletic figure. Khaemwase was a tall, well-built man, taking after his father in that respect, but he had the delicate facial features and long elegant hands of his mother Queen Isenofre. Those hands now lay folded and relaxed in his lap. His voice was soft and higher pitched than seemed natural for such a large man. His eyelashes were luxuriant and his arched brows, which naturally met above his nose, were plucked into fine, almost feminine lines.

Only a small number of men could claim to know the Prince and fewer still liked him, but then he had rarely allowed anyone to come close enough to see what Sunero could see. Here was a man with many faces, most of them private, some of them secret. To the world Khaemwase was a model son to his father. Being Sem Priest of Ptah in Mennefer as well as Controller of the Sanctuary of the Apis Bull, he had under his hand two of the richest cults outside the Holy City of Waset. Educated at Court alongside his brothers he had acquired a taste for learning, which he had continued to indulge in the Temple House of Life long after his siblings had finished with education altogether. His thirst for knowledge of all kinds had become legendary and he claimed that he was still learning. There probably had never been such an educated man. He was a collector of antiquarian books and a student of his family history. He was a patron of the arts with a particular feel for architecture both ancient and modern. He had been instrumental in the restoration of many monuments built by his most distant ancestors and had personally chosen the design for the new burial complex below the Temple of the Dead Apis. His had been the guiding hand behind the organisation of his father's many Jubilee celebrations as well as taking most seriously his position as priest of the god Ptah, the Great

Craftsman. But all this had not set him totally above or outside the ordinary world.

In Sunero's opinion, for what that was worth, Khaemwase understood more about everything than any man living. And he cared. If the Prince showed an interest in anything at all, that interest was genuine even in the most mundane of cases. He would make sure that he knew all there was to know about the matter and he was able to recall the most insignificant details years after the event. His intellect was vast. He held more information at his fingertips than Sunero would forget in a lifetime. Even now, after thirty years in the Prince's service, Sunero could not truthfully say that he liked his master. He respected him, he admired him, and in a way that he could not explain, he loved him, but Khaemwase was not a likeable man. And yet Sunero would have moved earth and sky at the Prince's command, though it might cost him his own life.

The Spy and the Count bowed on entering Khaemwase's presence. The Prince's casual gaze took in what they carried between them, the plain wooden box with its sloping lid, of the sort used by scribes as a portable desk, and the cylindrical leather document case slung over Sunero's shoulder.

'So,' the Prince said, 'you have decided at last to tell me. That, I take it, is why you are both here – you my faithful Spy and you my worthy Count.'

The two men bowed their agreement. 'Well then, let it be good. I want to know everything, from the very beginning. Let me see it, let me hear it, let me smell it for myself. Let me live through what you know. I have all the time in the world.'

With a glance at his friend, who nodded his agreement, Sunero opened the file box and brought out the first letter, the one that had started the adventure a quarter of a century ago.

*

The Scribe of Accounts in the Mansion of His Majesty, Hatiay, salutes the Tjaty of the Northern Realm, Sethi. Greetings, noble lord! This letter is to inform you of a situation that has arisen here concerning the storehouses of His Majesty, to whom be Life, Prosperity and Health.

Recently the Lady of the House, Takhenet, wife of the temple official, Simut, presented herself at the royal stores, demanding certain commodities in the name of her husband. Her demands being greatly in excess of her just allocation, the guardian of the stores refused to give her access. He reported the matter to his superior, the Overseer of the Royal Stores, Riya.

The woman Takhenet lodged a complaint with the said Riya as to the insolent manner of his underling and repeated her demands for certain goods to be released to her as of right. The Overseer was concerned that the woman seemed to think these things were due to her because, she said, her husband had always provided such goods for his family. Riya brought his suspicions to your humble servant and we arranged to inspect the private storerooms of the temple servant, Simut, who is at this time in the Northern Realm conducting a census of the herds of the god. We took an inventory of the contents, a copy of which is herewith enclosed. Though we found nothing that could be proved to have been taken illegally from the royal stores, we found Simut's storeroom to be filled with all sorts of goods and equipment that the woman could not explain. We left instruct-tions that nothing should be removed from the store until my Lord Paser might judge whether there is a case to answer.

However, My Lord the Tjaty Paser is most engaged with prepar-ations for His Majesty's Jubilee and has little time to spare for such matters. That being so, your humble servant and the Overseer of the Royal Stores, Riya, consider it appropriate that Lord Sethi should be informed. We are concerned that this matter, which may appear to be simply a case of one greedy woman overstepping her authority, has much deeper signif-icance. We are not in a position to demand an inventory of every royal storehouse in Waset but we are convinced that this might, in the end, be necessary. It is our opinion that we may have pulled back only a single layer of a problem that goes deep into the fabric of the system. We go so far as to say that we fear the integrity of His Majesty's private stores may have been compromised, though we have no proof at present that they have been violated.

We respectfully beg that our concerns be registered in the depart-mental archives of both Tjatys so that, should our fears be proved justif-iable, which may the gods forbid, then it may be seen that we did our duty and were vigilant in the care and conduct of our offices. All we have done has been done with the love of the Good God in our hearts.

The letter had borne the seal of the Mansion of His Majesty, the King's great mortuary temple in Waset. It was the same seal used by the Lord Tjia, who had been married to the King's own sister and who was at that time Superintendent of the Mansion. The letter had been placed among communications from other high-ranking officials and had been opened as a matter of priority so the secretary had not been able to hide it from the Tjaty Sethi. The scribe, Menna, felt aggrieved that he had been tricked into bringing what he considered to be an inconsequential matter to his master's attention but, as he later told Sunero, the Tjaty had taken it very casually.

'Perhaps there is more to this than you imagine, Menna,' the Tjaty had drawled. 'Perhaps we should investigate further.'

Menna felt that there was quite enough work to be dealt with concerning the administration of the North without the Tjaty taking on a sensitive case in the Southern Realm. 'But my Lord,' he protested, with temerity, 'This is not Your Lordship's province.'

'Perhaps not, but the letter is quite clear in explaining why my old friend Paser cannot deal with this. It is equally clear that the letter-writer has a genuine concern. We would be failing in our duty if we were to do nothing.'

'Hysterical nonsense,' Menna muttered under his breath.

'Eh? What did you say?' Sethi cupped a hand to his good ear.

Menna wanted to be rid of this tiresome business that threatened to distract his master's attention from more immediate and legitimate concerns. In spite of Sethi's protestations of friendship for his Southern counterpart, there was a well-known if unspoken rivalry between the two Tjatys. Paser was a companion of the King's youth, a man with the royal ear, and therefore a courtier in such high standing that even the Northern Tjaty acknowledged his superiority. Sethi's motives, in taking an interest in this southern parochial affair, were not entirely altruistic and so, Menna judged, were likely to lead to inter-departmental wrangling of the sort he could not bear to contemplate. He had to suggest a way out, a way in which his master would not lose face.

'I wondered, my lord, whether we might not pass on the respons-ibility to someone closer to the problem.'

'An excellent idea,' Sethi said with a smile, 'But to whom should we pass it on?' He put his hand to his chin and gazed at the ceiling as if seeking inspiration from a higher power.

There was a pause. The secretary had to let the Tjaty make the suggestion but when Sethi spoke Menna could not have been more surprised. 'I have it,' the Tjaty slapped his knee, 'The matter concerns the Royal Stores, if we are to believe this Hatiay. In this Jubilee Year it would seem wholly appropriate if a Royal commission looked into the matter. Yes, a letter to His Highness the Crown Prince, if you please Menna.'

*

Sunero took the copy of the Tjaty's letter from the file box.

The Tjaty of the Northern Realm, Governor of the Residence City, Sethi, pays his respects to His Royal Highness the King's Eldest Son, Ramesses, may he live, prosper and be healthy.

Having received a communication from the Southern City regard-ing the business of His Majesty's private Treasury at the Mansion, it is your servant's opinion that Your Highness might consider it worthy of his personal attention. Although we have received little in the way of evidence we consider that the concern shown by His Majesty's servants in bringing the matter to our notice warrants further investigation. The servants in the Royal employ in Waset are sure to appreciate Your Lordship's interest in their affairs, especially in this Jubilee Year. Thus we respectfully suggest that Your Highness might graciously condescend to head a board of inquiry into the situation.

'How comes that particular letter to be in your collection, Sunero?' asked the Prince, 'I assume even you did not have access to my brother's correspondence.'

'No, Sir, but the Tjaty's secretary, Menna, was so concerned that he might have broken open a hornets' nest that he did everything he could to cover himself. He wrote a letter on his own account and sent it, with a copy of his master's letter, to me.'

'Oho! I suppose you were already well known for your intelligence activities, but why should Menna risk his very comfortable position in such a way? Making illicit copies of official documents seems a rather risky business, wouldn't you say?'

'Menna was an old school friend of mine and we had been in fairly regular contact through work on Your Highness' behalf. He was a very worried man when he wrote that letter. He had hoped that the annoying business would have been buried and forgotten in the natural accumulation of correspondence, but then suddenly it was being made the basis of a full Royal Commission of Inquiry. He could foresee retribution falling in his direction once the Crown Prince realised that his time was being wasted. But then, when he had had a chance to re-read Hatiay's letter, he could almost feel the man's anxiety flowing from the papyrus. Perhaps there was something to be worried about after all, a sensitive matter that closely concerned the King. In that case, Menna considered that Crown Prince Ramesses was not the person to deal with it. He may have been ideally suited to his position as Commander in Chief of the army, but...' Sunero paused, wondering how much he dared say about his master's dead brother.

Khaemwase smiled, 'I know what you mean, Sunero. My dear brother was never comfortable with his role as Crown Prince for all that he held the position for more than twenty years. Strange as it may seem, I believe he was very self-conscious, almost shy. He knew where his skills lay and was confident, even bold, when working within his own capabilities, but when he had to step outside the security of the barracks or the training ground he was as unhappy as a fish on a sandbank. The military life suited him perfectly and I know he found fulfilment there. He was equally at ease discussing tactics with a general or logistics with a donkey handler, but in a room full of bureaucrats he felt inadequate and became tongue-tied. Officialdom intimidated him. He could never admit this failing, of course, for in the eyes of the King, our father, it would have been seen as a major disability in one destined for godhood. He would try to bluff his way out of any awkward situation but he convinced no one. I am afraid to say it, but Ramesses was not noted for his tact, his patience, nor, it has to be admitted, his intelligence. He was sincere in his love of the army and he was, without doubt, a gifted soldier, but in other areas of princecraft he was a great disappointment to His Majesty. You came to know him quite well, Sunero. You knew his ways. You were perhaps able to understand the man hiding behind the bluster.'

'Yes, Highness. The Crown Prince was an honest man. It was his misfortune to be pitted against some of the most cunning minds I have ever known.' Sunero shot a meaningful glance at the Count who smiled broadly.

'Truly,' Khaemwase said, 'an honest man! Yes, I think Ramesses would have appreciated that evaluation, even more so if you had called him an honest soldier. The army was really all he knew, and all he cared to know about. For him, the Waset affair was like going into battle in foreign territory with no plan of campaign and virtually no information about the size, weaponry or tactics of the enemy forces. No soldier would commit himself to such a dangerous venture. No wonder my brother was unhappy, and I can quite understand Menna's reservations. I take it you have his letter there. Let me hear it!'

The Tjaty's Scribe, Menna, greets the Agent of the King's Son Khaemwase, the Scribe Sunero. Hail to you my brother. In my capacity as secretary to His Excellency the Tjaty Sethi, I have received information which I think may be of interest to your master, the Prince Khaemwase. I enclose with this letter a copy of the communication recently received from one Hatiay, a Scribe of Accounts in the Mansion of the King in Waset. As you will see from the second letter enclosed, my master has passed on responsibility for this matter to His Highness the Crown Prince Ramesses, but I know that all matters concerning the King and the Royal Mansion are of interest to your lord. I hesitate to suggest that you should set this information before His Highness but I have an uneasy feeling that what may seem, at first reading, to be hysterical overreaction, may in fact turn out to have far-reaching implications. I leave the matter in your capable hands, to tell or not as you see fit. My master does not know that I am writing this letter, nor does he know of the copies I have made of his correspondence, so please, I beg you, keep my confidence.

Sunero had read Menna's letter and the copies of those from Hatiay and Sethi with growing interest. Menna was not noted for causing unnecessary fuss. He was an unimaginative sort who liked things straightforward and simple and hated anything unusual that threatened to upset his comfortable world, so if Menna was unhappy about the situation developing in Waset then it might well bear further investigation.

*

Replacing the letters in the file box, Sunero explained, 'I knew Your Highness was due to visit Waset shortly to proclaim the King's Jubilee. If Prince Ramesses was going to get there first I knew you would most certainly expect to be informed and would want to know as much as possible about the Crown Prince's business. It was my duty to find out what I could.'

'And as usual you were most conscientious in the performance of your duty, my good Sunero. I remember that meeting well and I recall most vividly that inventory that you insisted I should read.'

Sunero grinned and spared a sidelong glance at his companion who was smirking – there was no other word for the look on the Count's face.

'Yes,' the Prince was trying not to smile, 'It was a most amusing piece of literature. Tell me, my dear Count, how closely do you think the facts match my imagination?'

Still grinning, the Count nodded. 'It was a pretty unbelievable sight. When I first entered that storeroom I thought I would find in it much the same goods as in any domestic store. There were the usual sacks of grain, jars of oil and wine, bags of salt and bundles of leather, much as I expected, but the farther I went into the store, the more amazing it became. There was a box piled high with sandals, good leather sandals, of all sizes to fit children, men and women. I'd never seen so many in one place. The topmost sandals were quite new and one pair looked as if it had been made only the day before, but the rest. When I got closer I found that most of them were falling apart, the leather was so old it had perished. These were good quality sandals which had never been worn. They'd been acquired and stored, or hoarded I should say. No one ever benefited from them in any way. Then there was the linen. There were gowns and shawls, kilts and loincloths, all neatly folded away in clothes presses but no one would ever wear them. Some of them would have cracked along the creases if you'd tried to unfold them. There was more clothing stored away there than any family could hope to need. There was a pile of bed sheets too, beautiful things of the finest weave. The first one on the pile was white and smooth but towards the bottom the cloth was yellowed and dusty and there were signs that mice had been nibbling at it. The thing that really astounded me was the harness. There was a great tangle of it; bridles, plough and cart harness, donkey saddles, mostly unusable because they hadn't been oiled properly. In fact none of it had received any attention since the day it was first put into the store and besides, Takhenet never owned the donkeys or oxen to warrant half as much tackle. She was just keeping things for the sake of possessing them. She can't possibly have used a fraction of what she had gathered, nor hoped ever to use it. It was just a collection, a sad, pitiful collection.'

'No wonder Hatiay was suspicious,' the Prince murmured, 'And yet you say there was nothing to suggest that this sad woman was a thief?'

Sunero took up the story. 'I studied that inventory. I read it through so many times that I could almost write it down from memory. It was an incredible list but nothing on it was directly traceable to the Royal Stores apart from the sacks of grain, which had been issued legitimately as part of the man Simut's salary. But I could not imagine how such a collection of goods could have been accumulated, knowing the level of the family's income. Vast amounts of grain or copper or bronze must have been bartered in exchange for the leather and linen goods alone. Even allowing for the time over which the collection had been made, it still represented far more wealth than Simut's position could have merited. Hatiay had stumbled on a real puzzle.'

'And the nature of that puzzle?' the Prince asked.

'Well, Your Highness, assuming the goods used to barter for all these useless luxuries had come from an official source then a shortage should have been noticed or a deficit recorded in some other area, and it was no small amount we were considering. There are always losses from the temple stores; some are accidental like the breakage of wine jars through mishandling, some are natural like insect or rodent damage, and some result from intentional pilfering. But none of the records which Hatiay and Riya had sifted through had revealed losses of the level to account for Takhenet's collection. The value, even spread over a period of ten or fifteen years, was enormous and way beyond Simut's expectations. Only the Royal Stores could have provided such wealth and yet, there was no record of losses on that scale. There remained one possibility and this was so unimaginable that Hatiay began to get really worried. The only source of riches in such quantity was the Treasury of the King himself, His Majesty's personal and private strongrooms at the Mansion.

'Of course Hatiay had not been able to check the records of the Treasury. He tried to talk with Kenro, the Chief Scribe, but Kenro laughed at the very suggestion that he should allow Hatiay access to the King's private records. The Chief Custodian of the Treasury, Harmose, got very angry when Hatiay merely suggested that he might review his security arrangements. Hatiay was obstructed at every move and the more obstruct-tion he found the more determined he became that he was right. It took a brave man to write that letter to the Tjaty Sethi and a bold man to use the Seal of the Mansion so that the letter received priority attention when it arrived in Mennefer. Hatiay was a good man.'

There was a hint of sadness in Sunero's voice as he remembered his friend. Hatiay also had deserved to know the truth but had passed over to the West only the previous year without having had his professional curiosity satisfied. Hatiay's most useful years had been spent profitably in Khaemwase's service but, however much wealth and prestige he had accumulated for himself, the Scribe's knowledge that he had a significant matter of business outstanding had always gnawed at his heart like a determined mouse chewing at a cellar door.

Khaemwase also remembered Hatiay with kindness. 'Good men are hard to find,' he said almost to himself.

The light was fading now. Sunero could imagine the dilemma of the Prince's servants in the outer hall, wondering whether they dared defy their master and bring in lamps. Khaemwase sensed his concern. 'You too are a good man, Sunero, the best. Go now, have your evening meal. The story must continue tomorrow. I shall not die just yet.'

Sunero walked through the garden court of the Prince's residence, his hands clasped behind his back, his head bowed. The Count walked beside him with a jauntier step.

'How can you be so cheerful?' the Spy turned on his companion. 'Can't you see what's happening?'

'I see a man who is bored with life, if that's what you mean.'

'Bored to death!'

'But we've just rekindled an interest for him. He'll not go to Osiris before he's heard our tale in full. We can spin it out for days.'

'What difference will a few days make? He's still going to die.'

The Count shrugged, 'Who can tell? Our story might just bring him out of his lethargy. We can but try.' He slapped Sunero on the back. 'Come home with me. I've a good jar of wine just begging to be opened.'

'Won't your wife mind?'

'Remember who she is, who she was. She's part of all this.'

Chapter Two

'So you have come back,' the Prince looked vaguely surprised as the two men entered. He had left instructions with his Steward, Montmose, that they should be admitted as soon as they arrived. It was already late in the morning. He had almost given up hope. Rising from a respectful bow, the Count looked the Prince straight in the eye.

For a long moment Khaemwase locked gazes with the Count, trying to assess his mood. He had not known this man as long as he had his faithful Spy. There were still some facets of his character that surprised him, still some rough edges that grated against royal sensibilities. In earlier days, Khaemwase would have been angered by such insolence, but now he could read something in the man's face that softened the anger. The air of confrontation was cultivated to enrage, to challenge, to stir up emotions which Khaemwase thought he had suppressed long ago. The Count was deliberately risking his master's displeasure. Even Sunero faced his lord with head held high. They had no concern for themselves at this time. All their attention was for the Prince. They were willing to chance his momentary displeasure in their attempt to prolong his life.

Khaemwase had rarely loved anyone or anything to the extent of being prepared to risk his very life for that love. It was difficult for a prince to comprehend the feelings of ordinary folk, though Khaemwase had tried more than most to understand the ways of his people. Sunero and the Count had been of great assistance to him in this learning process but the Prince had always been an observer rather than a participant. When real danger had threatened he had not recognised it and, more than once, his faithful servants had had to rescue him from himself as well as from the painful realities of the common life. He owed them both more than he could ever admit, certainly more than they would accept. He was their lord; they were his servants. Their situations had been ordained by the gods and none would dream of challenging the divine order of Maat. But they were prepared to challenge the Prince's human decision to die, because they cared. This depth of feeling was unfamiliar to Khaemwase and for this, if for nothing else, the story-tellers deserved his attention. They were, as always, working in his best interests so he could forgive their boldness, bordering on insolence, for the while.

The Prince waved to the chairs which he had ordered to be placed close to his couch and Sunero and the Count sat down. 'Well, get on with it,' Khaemwase said with just a hint of snappishness. It was the most animation he had shown for days. Sunero felt his heart leap. Perhaps the Count was right. Perhaps they could yet restore Khaemwase's interest in life. He opened the file box and drew forth the next relevant document.

'Your Highness will remember this,' he said. 'This is the commission which I took with me to Waset at Your Highness' command.'

'Ah, yes. As I recall, we decided that my dear departed brother could not be trusted to sniff out a rotten egg in a flower garden. I wanted to be kept informed of the case and who better to send than my own Spy?'

Sunero bowed his head acknowledging his master's implicit praise. The trust that the Prince had shown in him over the years was gratifying, and to know that he had been appreciated was a reward in itself. The commission had given Sunero broad powers. He could requisition transport in the Prince's name and he could use the Royal messenger service to send his reports to Khaemwase in Mennefer. He could obtain food and lodging on demand at any estate of the Royal Domain. He was given the names of certain officials within the administrative departments in Waset who might be of assistance in his inquiries, with separate letters of authority. He was even given an introduction to the Prince's kinsman, the Lord Tjia, Superintendent of the King's Mansion Temple, which would have admitted him to the highest level of the local administration. Khaemwase had warned him that the ageing Lord Tjia would not take kindly to interference in Mansion affairs, whether real or perceived, so Sunero should use this power sparingly and only in greatest need. His access to Temple records was limited but the Prince's warrant gave him total freedom to talk with anyone in the Royal service who might be involved in the matter, though he was instructed, above all else, not to become involved in the legal case itself.

Ostensibly Sunero was in the Holy City to prepare the way for his master's visit and as the Prince's Agent in Mennefer he had limited authority over the household servants, clerks and other workers in Khaem-wase's country estate outside Waset. His role was not stated explicitly since in Waset his position was unofficial, but all of the

Prince's people accepted his presence without question and referred all enquiries about him to their superiors. Khaemwase had always been able to instil perfect loyalty and discretion in his employees. If Sunero was to be given unprecedented freedom of movement and access to information the Prince was confident that his Spy would not abuse these privileges.

At about the same time as Sunero had been boarding a boat in Mennefer, the Scribe Accountant of the Temple Herds, Simut, was also on his way south in response to the letter he had received from his brother. This was the next papyrus to be brought from Sunero's file box. Khaemwase's eyebrows rose and he looked questioningly at the Count. 'How have you obtained a copy of that letter?'

'Not a copy, Highness. This is the original. I found it among my brother's papers and, knowing how Sunero likes to tie up loose ends, I gave it to him when we moved to Mennefer.'

'I see. So this really will be the whole story – this time.'

'The whole story, Sir, my word on it.'

*

The Chief Designer of the Mansion, Amenhotep, sends greetings to his brother the Scribe Accountant of the Herds of Amen, Simut. Brother, an urgent matter has arisen which demands your presence in Waset at once. Your wife has been officious in her dealings with the guardians of the Royal Stores and in consequence charges of misappropriation and fraudulent conversion of state property are to be lodged against her. Your storerooms have been searched but not yet sealed, as the Scribe Hatiay could not find the proof he sought. But it is our concern that your wife, by her intemperate actions, may have compromised the family's reputation. I will do my best to represent your wife and protect the family name but she will not listen to me as she would to her husband. Come home, dear Brother. Come home as soon as you can.

While Simut and Sunero spent their days travelling with varying degrees of impatience, matters in Waset were gathering to a head. Hatiay had made a thorough search through all the records of the Royal Stores and had compiled a list of goods unaccounted for. He then compared this list with the strange inventory from Simut's storehouse. The resulting assembly of possible misappropriations was most unsatisfactory as it included sacks of grain, bags of salt, spools of thread and jars of oil, none of which bore any identifying marks, and their provenance could not be confirmed. The evidence he was clutching at, as a drowning man will clutch at a reed, was circumstantial at best. Hatiay suffered several sleepless nights during which, in his mind's eye, he turned the evidence over and over, looking at it from all possible directions, trying to pull the strands together into a believable fabric of proof. Nothing he saw, either in his waking dreams or the cluttered reality of Simut's storeroom, came close to proving Takhenet guilty. And yet, Hatiay held the gut-wrenching belief that she, or more probably her husband, was concealing a crime so heinous, so huge, that it was almost unimaginable. A crime that could not be imagined was likely to go undetected. As his sleeplessness continued and the shadows beneath his eyes grew darker, Hatiay began to take the matter personally.

When the messenger of the Tjaty Sethi arrived from the north and presented his credentials to Mahu, the Deputy of the Mansion, Hatiay and Riya were summoned to explain themselves. Though Mahu was put out at finding himself less well-informed than his subordinates, and having to admit as much before the Tjaty's representative, he was quick to see the implications of a Royal Inquiry. Hatiay later told Sunero that he had begun to sweat when he heard the news that Prince Ramesses had been appointed to head the inquiry. He had never imagined that his letter would have had such dramatic results. And what would become of him if he had wasted the time of so many high-ranking officials with his petty worries? He brazened it out, persuading Mahu that he was on the verge of uncovering solid evidence that would justify the Crown Prince's presence in Waset. The result was a summons issued against the woman, Takhenet, calling her to present herself, with her advisers as necessary, in the Mansion Hall of Justice the following day. There they would be told of the Tjaty's decision. There Takhenet would hear who were to be her judges.

*

'And what was the woman's reaction to that news?' the Prince asked.

'She was terrified,' answered the Count. 'For the first time ever I think she was struck dumb, which was probably just as well since she would surely have condemned herself beyond redemption if she had found her tongue.'

'And her husband?'

'He hadn't yet reached Waset. It was his brother who did all the talking. He stayed pretty calm in the circumstances but when he got home he was furious. I heard him come in. I'm surprised the whole neighbour-hood didn't hear him. I just sat in the shadows halfway down the stairs. I saw and heard it all.'

*

Amenhotep slammed the door behind him. 'May the gods preserve us from meddling princes!'

'What's happened?' Rai asked. Her anxiety had been growing ever since her husband had left for the Mansion that morning. It was now past sunset and the evening meal remained untouched. When Ameny missed his food there had to be an important reason.

'Tell me,' she persisted, trying to halt his angry prowling around the room. 'Have the judges been appointed?'

'Yes they have and that's the trouble. His Royal sodding-Highness, Crown Prince Kiss-my-butt Ramesses is to preside!'

Rai's jaw dropped and her hand fell from Amenhotep's arm as he shrugged away and kicked viciously at a footstool. The fragile little thing smashed against the wall and fell to the floor with two of its legs broken.

'What does he know about civil law? What does he know about the system here? What does he know about anything? He's a soldier by all that's holy!'

A leather cushion followed the stool, its seams splitting and leaving a trail of sawdust. Rai hurried to protect a treasured alabaster lamp on its stand which seemed to be next in line for her husband's foot. 'Ameny, don't! Please! We must make the best of it. Losing your temper won't help!'

'It's so damned frustrating!' he yelled, but his movement slowed and the lamp was saved. 'It's bad enough that our stupid sister should have got us into this situation but at least with a local judge we should have been able to tidy things away quickly. Now His idiotic Highness will want to go over everything from the very beginning and we'll have to explain how two and two don't make five.'

'Why is the Crown Prince taking charge?' Rai asked.

'A whim, I shouldn't wonder. Princes don't need reasons. It's coming up for the King's Jubilee. It's time to remind people who's the Royal Heir. Making a name for himself, that's what it's all about. It's not even as if he cares about us. He just wants to be seen doing the sort of thing a Crown Prince ought to do.'

'So, it may not actually be such a bad thing,' Rai said carefully. 'If he only wants to be seen doing his duty he may not take much interest in the case itself. He could just be a figurehead for the court, a non-participating judge.'

'He hasn't got the intelligence to participate. His head's been softened by too much weapons practice. But he could interfere, prolong things, stick his nose in at precisely the wrong moment. It would be just our luck to have him chance upon a flaw in our case.'

'It's a good job Prince Khaemwase hasn't heard about it then,' Rai said softly.

Amenhotep stopped his pacing and looked at his wife with furrowed brows. 'There is that, I suppose,' he said. 'Khaemwase as judge would have put the lid on Takhenet's coffin before we ever got to court.' The Crown Prince's younger brother had already gained a considerable reputation in Waset before it was made public that he was to organise the royal Jubilee celebrations. Local officials, especially those in the temple administration where both Amenhotep and Simut worked, were in awe of Prince Khaemwase's ability to see straight through any obfuscation, and not a little intimidated by his directness. Yes, Khaemwase as Takhenet's judge would spell disaster for the family.

'Well then,' Rai said in the most reasonable tone she could muster, 'Look at it this way. Things could be a lot worse. If we have to have a royal judge then with Prince Ramesses we have at least a chance.'

'That's true,' Amenhotep put his arm about his wife's shoulders. 'You're right as usual. If only Simut had married a woman as sensible as you, then we wouldn't be in this mess.'

'But since we are in it, we must do our best to clear it up. We have the children to consider. The family name must be cleared.'

Over his wife's head, Amenhotep continued to frown. He knew the impending court case was not as simple as Rai believed. Only he and Simut could appreciate its full implications and there were aspects of the case that neither brother had been foolish enough to confide to his wife.

Rai went on, 'And Simut could be home tomorrow, or the next day at the latest. He'll have had your letter. He'll probably be preparing his case on the boat.'

Yes, Amenhotep thought, *he'll have the letter but I couldn't write everything I wanted to say. I hope he has realised what the real problem is. This could be a dangerous homecoming for Simut.*

*

'And was the worthy Simut long in making his appearance?' the Prince asked.

'He was already much closer to Waset than we imagined,' the Count chuckled.

'What is so amusing?' Khaemwase sensed an entertaining anecdote. 'Come, my dear Count, do not stint. You promised me the whole story.'

*

At about the time that Amenhotep was thinking about his brother, the boat's captain was explaining to Simut just how dangerous his home-coming could be. 'The sandbars now, you need to know the River well to negotiate the Waset sandbars after dark.'

'But you were only telling me yesterday, Captain, that no one knew the waters hereabouts better than you. In fact, it was on account of your acknowledged expertise that I chose to travel in your craft. Surely you were not exaggerating your own competence?' Simut said, his tongue dripping with implied flattery.

The skipper opened his mouth then closed it again while he re-considered his reply. Simut forced himself to keep a pleasant, relaxed smile on his face while behind this mask he was seething with impatience. He had personal experience of the waters at Waset and had negotiated the river by night on many occasions, albeit in the family's small rowing boat. He knew the boatman was trying to raise the price of this already expensive journey.

He had commandeered the craft in the name of his employer, who was no less than the god Amen-Ra himself, but would have to find the bulk of the hire out of his own storehouses since he was not travelling on official temple business. But he had to get back to Waset as soon as possible. They were less than two night-hours sailing time from the town quay but the usual practice was to seek a mooring at the River's edge during the hours of darkness. Simut was prepared to pay extra if the captain would only go on and he knew that the crew would prefer to stop over for the night in the Southern City rather than in the middle of nowhere with nothing but roosting waterfowl for company. He was perfectly aware that the skipper knew his own worth and was expecting to haggle, driving a hard bargain in order to maintain his professional standing, but the captain's next bargaining ploy had him gasping at the man's audacity.

'There's the hippos', the boatman said with a sly smile.

'Hippos?' Simut almost squeaked in surprise. 'Surely that is not a serious concern?'

'You never can tell. Those beasts come out to eat after sunset. They swim under the water so's you can't see 'em. Then they comes up under those floating mats of water plants. If one comes up under your bow, it can smash the hull in. Alongside and the wash'll swamp you. At the stern and the steering oar could be snapped like a straw.'

Simut schooled his face again. He could not remember the last time he had seen a hippopotamus this close to Waset, let alone heard of one sinking a boat. The likelihood of them encountering such a danger would seem to be remote, to put it mildly, but he would have to give way to the captain's ploy. He suggested an amount which he considered suitable in the circumstances. The captain looked offended but the bargaining had begun in earnest. When finally they agreed on what Simut knew was an extortionate fee, he could feel nothing but relief. He left the final details to his secretary who was already tut-tutting over his master's casual agreement to guarantee future commissions for the boatman. There was little hope that such a promise could be kept, given Simut's position. An accountant of the Temple herds had no authority over the Temple's transport requirements. While the skipper made a great show of setting crewmen with torches on 'hippo watch', Simut retired to the aft cabin to study his brother's letter.

The meagre oil lamp, the flaring torches and a pale half-moon gave ample light but Simut looked at the papyrus sheet without reading it. He already knew its contents by heart. He also knew only too well what his brother had meant him to read in between the lines. The bare facts, as any-one could have read, were that his wife Takhenet had been accused of mis-using his authority in his absence. She had been drawing extra supplies from the Royal stores which, in moderation, might have been overlooked. Simut, however, knew his wife and could all too well imagine the high-handed way in which she would have made her demands. Her overbearing manner, at times downright patronising, had won her no friends among the other wives. It was probably another woman who had informed on her. He had known that leaving her in control of the supplies during his trip to the North was risky but he could not refuse such an important commission. He had thought about asking Amenhotep to look after his affairs in his absence but Takhenet would have been offended by the mere suggestion that she needed a guardian. He had worried from the moment his boat had pulled away from the quayside in Waset about what Takhenet might do while he was away.

Simut's wife had always thought, and frequently said, that she had married beneath her. Her family had kept their distance after the wedding as a sign of their disapproval even though it was their somewhat straitened circumstances that had led to the arrangement of the match. They were also rather embarrassed at having off-loaded a potentially devastating drain on their remaining resources on to the unsuspecting Simut. Takhenet's acquisitive nature was well known to all except her new husband, and it was not long before he too realised what a problem that could be. Simut had managed to keep Takhenet's ambition within bounds by maintaining his family to a standard which she could not fault. The very fact of his being chosen to carry out the census of herds in the god's northern estates was a double-edged blade. It raised his status in her eyes but also gave her the opportunity to put on further airs.

Amenhotep had volunteered to keep an eye on things and Simut trusted his brother implicitly, but Amenhotep and Takhenet had hated each other from the moment they first met. Ameny had tried to dissuade his younger brother from what he saw as a disastrous marriage. Now, even he would have to admit that it had worked out better than could have been hoped, but only because Simut had been able to provide over and above the usual line of comforts and luxuries for his demanding wife. That too was down to Ameny for he had shared with Simut the Secret, which was at the very heart of their success and prosperity. It was the threat that Takhenet, by her ill-considered actions, might unwittingly reveal the Secret to the world that was driving Simut homewards as fast as the north wind and a grasping ship's captain could bear him.

*

'So, at last,' the Prince sighed with satisfaction, 'The Secret. And when will we be admitted to the knowledge of this Secret?'

'In time, Sir. It would spoil the story to reveal all now,' the Count said.

'I suppose so,' the Prince sighed again. 'But now I am hungry and I am sure you two would wish to retire for some refreshment. Return this afternoon. The story must go on.'

As Sunero and the Count bowed themselves out, the Spy could hardly contain his glee. In the anteroom he grasped the Count's forearm. 'Did you hear him? He said he's hungry. He hasn't shown any interest in food for days. I think you may be right. We might save him yet.'

'Only if he wants to be saved. He's already sixty years old after all. Perhaps he just doesn't want to go on.'

Sunero refused to be downhearted. He signalled to the Prince's Steward who approached and bowed. The man's brow wore a permanent furrow of concern for his master. Khaemwase certainly had the knack of inspiring loyalty if not affection in his servants.

'Is His Highness all right?' the Steward asked as if fearing the reply he might receive.

'Yes, Montmose,' Sunero said with a grin, 'he's asking for food.'

Montmose's frown was instantly replaced by the raised brows and wide eyes of amazement, then he pulled himself together.

'Food! Food for His Highness!' he shouted, 'Now! Hurry ! Where is everyone?' and he bustled off to see that suitable delicacies were pro-duced to tempt his master's appetite.

Having followed the Steward to the kitchens, Sunero and the Count abstracted a jar of beer, some bread and a pot of cheese and took their simple meal into the garden court. They made their way to a small pavilion where ancient grapevines grew in a curtain between slender, reeded columns. They sat in the shade while drowsy bees buzzed around the flowers of convolvulus that threaded their tendrils in and out of the vines above them. They ate in companionable silence, each thinking his own thoughts, entwined in his own memories, and then they slept, leaning against the painted columns.

In his private quarters, the Prince also ate, picking the flesh from a grilled pigeon and selecting the plumpest grapes from a bowl of fruit. He ate with a distracted air, his mind far away in time and distance. The story that was unfolding had revived his own memories of that eventful year, the thirtieth of his father's reign. Much had happened since then but that particular year had been of great personal significance to Khaemwase. For so long he had lived in the shadow of his older brothers. After the obligatory royal education at the Mennefer military academy and several seasons spent on campaign with his father, even the King had to admit that Khaemwase's heart was not inclined towards soldiering. While his brothers had continued to make their names in the army he had acquired other skills and though they had derided him for his bookish nature, he only awaited the opportunity to prove that his time had not been wasted.

He had been appointed to the priesthood of the Apis temple when he was only sixteen, but it was not until the King asked him to take responsibility for the Jubilee celebrations that he had been called upon to use the talents he had developed. For him those years in the shadows had been formative and satisfying in a way that none of his siblings could ever understand. Like a butterfly breaking out from the pupa, fully formed, perfect, mature, Khaemwase had emerged as a personality of forceful character and immense superiority which quite overawed his brothers. Even people like Sunero, who had some inkling of the Prince's true nature, had been taken by surprise. Perhaps the only person who had never under-estimated Khaemwase's potential was the King himself.

'And now', the Prince said to himself, 'I am dying while my father goes on, apparently immortal. All that authority he gave me, the education he encouraged, the trust he showed in me, is it all to go for nothing? In the end, the Crowns of the Two Lands will go to one of those meat-headed soldiers whom I have always despised. But at least I have lived, and learned, and loved. I have had a fuller life than any of them. That is all I can expect. The gods never intended that I should be King.'

However lightly the Crowns might sit upon the brow of the King, his son knew that he would find their burden less easy to bear. Royal birth was not a guarantee of kingly qualities. The King had already experienced the truth of this in his four eldest sons, each nominated in his turn as Royal Heir. He had tried to mould and shape them in his image, to secure his family's divine destiny. By inconsiderately pre-deceasing him, each Crown Prince in turn had failed his father. Now that Khaemwase held the unenviable position of Royal Heir, the King had hoped that the succession was in safe if unwilling hands. Khaemwase realised, with the suddenness of a lightning flash, that the gods had never blessed him with a vision of himself wearing the Double Crown. Perhaps they were not as cruel as he imagined. He had served Ptah, the Great Artificer, for more than forty years. His son Hori had followed his path to become High Priest of Ptah and was content in the god's service. Perhaps the reward for their devotional life was for the family not to be burdened with the Kingship.

As for his oldest son, Ramesses, who hoped with a passion to be King some day, Khaemwase could never make him understand the awesome responsibilities that went with the Kingship, responsibilities to family, people, country and gods. And such musing was of academic interest only, for the King continued to thrive. Young Ramesses was too unimaginative to see beyond the trappings of power. He was in love with superficialities. The truth was too painful to explain and too complex for him to understand. Khaemwase found himself feeling sorry for the boy – no, not a boy, Ramesses was past forty years old and had children of his own. His resentment was understandable to Khaemwase who had suffered the same feelings of frustration and bewilderment at that age. And still the King lived.

How many other lives had been touched by the King's own boundless enthusiasm for life? How many spirits had been crushed by the King's overwhelming personality? How many hopes had been dashed? How many futures blighted? And the King lived on. But Khaemwase would have the last word in this particular struggle. He would die when he decided he had lived long enough, and in a manner and place of his own choosing. For once, his father would be powerless. Khaemwase's only regret was that he would not be able to observe the effects of this, his last defiance.

Young Ramesses was destined for disappointment, but he had had long enough already to prepare for it. If he had squandered his time in dreams of greatness then his was a wasted life and Khaemwase hated waste. The Crown Prince felt a momentary regret on behalf of his son's son, brought up in his father's beliefs and with all his father's expectations. It had been cruel of Young Ramesses to feed the boy's hopes and dreams when the King alone could make those dreams come true and that only by his death. With more than a twinge of guilt, Khaemwase remembered that he had not always been as caring as he might have been of his own children so he was hardly in a position to pass judgement on the way Young Ramesses had raised his son. While

Hori would genuinely mourn his father's passing, his soldier brother would regret Khaenwase's death for very different reasons. Young Ramesses took after the King in ambition, though in intelligence he was more like his namesake, Khaemwase's dead brother, and he would never understand his father's meek acceptance of death. He knew that if the Crown Prince died before the King, the position of Royal Heir would fall to another of the King's sons, and the succession would pass out of his line forever. And the King was alive still.

The fruit had little flavour. The meat seemed dry and the wine tasted tart. Even the little pleasures of life were waning. He would be glad to relinquish this earthly existence whose variety and novelty had long ago dwindled to mediocrity. If only he could be sure there were new sensations to be enjoyed in the afterlife. What a cruel joke it would be if, after a barely endurable mortal life, there was nothing beyond but more of the same. Perhaps the King's divinity gave him privileged information about what awaited him on the other side of the Western Horizon. Perhaps that was why he was delaying his journey to the Fields of Ra. Perhaps immortality was his reward for living life to the full, for, to be sure, the King still lived.

Khaemwase sighed, leaned back in his chair and closed his eyes. He could let go of life now, if he so wished. He could feel his spirit hovering at his side. The ties that bound them together as a single entity were stretched so very thin that the slightest movement, the softest breath could break them. It would take but a thought. Then the picture of the Count's insolent face came unbidden into Khaemwase's mind and his eyes snapped open. There was still something that he had to know. He knew his life would be incomplete without this knowledge. An incomplete life was a wasted life, and Khaemwase hated waste. The Prince would live, at least long enough to complete his education.

And the King would live forever.

Chapter Three

Sunero awoke with a start as some small creature ran across his leg. His involuntary exclamation roused the Count who was instantly awake.

'What is it? Scorpion?'

'No, lizard I think,' Sunero brushed away imagined footprints from his shin. Then he remembered, 'We left the file box in the Prince's room.'

The Count was unperturbed. 'Don't worry. He won't read anything unless we show it to him first. He doesn't want the story spoiled. He won't cheat.'

'Can you be sure of that?'

'Sure as I am of anything. But if you're worried we'd better get back to him.'

They stood up and dusted off their kilts before searching out a water jar so they could wash and make themselves presentable. When they entered the Prince's presence chamber he was waiting for them, im-patiently drumming the fingers of one hand in the palm of the other. The file box was just as they had left it.

'So let me see, where were we?' Khaemwase said, giving them barely a moment to collect their thoughts. 'A Royal Inquiry had been ordered with my dear brother named as chief judge and the worthy Simut was hurrying home to limit the damage done by his wife.'

'Yes,' the Count continued, 'he arrived about midnight. His hammering on the door was enough to wake the dead but then he knew the old doorkeeper was almost stone deaf and he was in quite a state of anxiety himself. When Amenhotep took him into his private workroom I crept downstairs and listened at the door.'

*

Amenhotep embraced Simut and urged him to sit down and take some refreshment before they started to talk. Rai served her husband's brother with sharp-tasting pomegranate wine before tactfully leaving the room. She knew their discussion would go on late into the night and she was not needed.

Simut had hardly cleared his mouth before asking, 'How much do they know, Ameny? Tell me the worst.'

Amenhotep patted his brother's shoulder. 'Don't worry too much, Simy,' he said, using the family nickname bestowed on Simut years ago by their sister, now dead. 'Takhenet still knows nothing and I think we might be able to explain the so-called evidence as long as she can be persuaded to back down.'

'So, she's been pushing her weight around again, has she? I guessed as much,' Simut sighed. 'What's the damage?'

'From the beginning?' Amenhotep asked.

'That would be best. I'm sure I can imagine much of it but I need to know the details.'

Amenhotep took a long slow breath before starting his story.

All temple and government employees received payment for their services in the form of rations drawn from the official stores. The higher a man's standing, the greater the value of the goods to which he was entitled. He could choose to have part of his entitlement in luxury goods such as fine linen, spices, sweet oils or domestic equipment of the very best quality. Takhenet had been well provided with such luxuries throughout her married life and she had always believed – and the brothers hoped she would continue to believe – that such things were appropriate remuneration for her husband's job as a senior accountant in the Temple of Amen-Ra.

While Simut had been employed in the North, organising the Jubilee census of herds, Takhenet had gone to the store-keepers of the magazines at the Temple of Ipet Esut with a list of her requirements which she considered to be no more than her due. The storekeepers had laughed in her face. Takhenet was not one to take such an insult lightly. She made a special trip across the River to confront the senior storekeeper of the Mansion, the King's great mortuary temple, and complained of the insolence shown to her by his junior officials. Riya was a short, portly man, very full of his own importance and contemptuous of women in general. Takhenet's stridency in her repeated claims that it was her right to have such things quickly hardened Riya's attitude towards her. Since he was also of a devious nature, he placated Takhenet with soft words and promises of prompt action against the wretches who had slighted her. She had returned home almost mollified but without any of the things she had so desperately wanted from the temple magazines.

Meanwhile, Riya set to work to investigate Takhenet's claims that she was accustomed to having such goods from the official stores. He found several wives of other temple employees who were only too willing to testify to the high standard of living enjoyed by Simut's family. Envy and resentment at Takhenet's haughty treatment of her equals made it easy for Riya to find people willing to bear witness against her. He had taken his informants before Hatiay, Chief Recording Scribe of the warehouses, and after half a day closeted in the scribe's office, the two men had emerged with enough evidence to obtain a warrant to search Simut's personal storerooms.

'When was that?' Simut asked.

'The day I wrote you the letter,' Amenhotep replied. 'The first we knew of the business was when Hatiay arrived with two Medjay policemen and a checklist of things he claimed were missing from the royal stores. Takhenet at least had the sense to call for me to come and witness the search. She had that right.'

'What did you do?'

'What could I do? I had to let them carry out their search, but they didn't get into the inner store. Even Takhenet hasn't realised that it's bigger on the outside than on the inside. But there was enough in the front storeroom to arouse their suspicions.'

'There's nothing there they can trace?'

'I hope not, after all the trouble we've taken. But even I was surprised at some of the stuff your wife has stowed away in there. What does she want with it all? When could she ever hope to use it?'

Simut bent forward, his elbows resting on his knees, his head in his hands. 'Takhenet, what have you done?'

'I'll tell you what she's been doing,' Amenhotep went on relentlessly. 'She's been trading off all our carefully chosen goods so she can stockpile a load of stuff which she's never needed and is never likely to use. And don't tell me you didn't know about it, Simy. She must have been doing this for years. Some of those sandals are already perishing through age though they've never been worn.'

'What did Hatiay say?'

'He was as surprised as I was. He was also annoyed that there was nothing he could point to as having come from the royal stores. But the contents of that storeroom would look suspicious even to the most simple-minded peasant. Hatiay took an inventory and went off to check it against the official stores' records. He promised he'd put in a report to the Tjaty and that's what he did, only it seems he also sent a copy to the Tjaty's office in Per-Ramesse. So it's turned into a national scandal instead of being kept as a purely local affair.'

'What happens next? When does the investigation start?' Simut asked anxiously.

'The judges were appointed today,' Amenhotep said.

His brother's voice, suddenly softer, warned Simut that there was more bad news. He looked up, his eyes dull, his eyelids heavy through worry and lack of sleep, and almost whispered, 'Tell me.'

'Prince Ramesses has become interested in the case. He will preside over the court.'

Simut's shoulders sagged. 'We're lost,' he said in a dreadful matter-of-fact tone.

'No, we're not.' Amenhotep snapped. 'There's a lot to be done but we can sort it all out if we're sensible. As long as they don't find the inner store there's nothing in your possession that they can trace back to the Mansion and even if they could track down some of the stuff we've already disposed of, it won't appear on their lists because it didn't come from the regular sources. We've got to disguise some of Takhenet's hoard. We can't have the inquiry asking questions about how she acquired the things she traded for all the stuff she's accumulated. We'll have to downplay the value of those goods, too. We'll get invoices, bills of sale, receipts. We'll explain away as much as we can but ...'

'But Takhenet will have to know!'

'Oh no, Simy, there's no way that woman can be let into the Secret.'

'She's my wife.'

'That's your fault,' Amenhotep said with brutal honesty. 'You have to keep the pact agreed long before she became your wife, and if it means Takhenet becoming a laughing stock because of her *collection*, then so be it. I haven't even told Rai though I know she could keep her mouth shut. Takhenet can't be trusted and you know that perfectly well.'

'She'll die of embarrassment,' Simut moaned and Amenhotep watched in dismay as tears welled in his brother's eyes. Even after all these years and all the trouble she had caused him, Simut still loved his wife. Amenhotep relented and placed a hand on the younger man's shoulder. 'We'll do our best, Simy, I promise you. It won't be easy and we'll have to have our story so well-rehearsed that it's Crown-Prince-proof, but I doubt it can be done.'

Simut nodded. He had to be realistic and they were short of time. 'How can we get the paperwork done without giving away too much?'

'I've been thinking about that. Hari has nearly finished his training. He's a skilled enough scribe already. He can draw up suitable documents. It's time we let the boys into the Secret. We're neither of us getting any younger. We'll have to pass it on soon.'

'My sons aren't old enough to be trusted with anything so important.'

'But my boys are. Let's face it Simy, we need to tell someone. If things go wrong you and I might not live to profit any more from our knowledge.'

Here Simut put his foot down. 'No, Ameny, we can't tell your boys everything until we can tell my sons too. That's only fair. Tell them as much as they need to know to help us out of this situation but the Secret must remain a secret for the time being.'

Reluctantly Amenhotep agreed. 'In the morning then. We'll meet here first thing in the morning.'

*

'So, even then they would not reveal the secret to their own sons. No wonder it has been so well kept since,' the Prince could not help but be impressed. 'And what's this about an inner store? Did I hear you correctly, Count, that Simut's storehouse was larger on the outside than on the inside? Explain this to me.'

'It was ingenious Sir. Of course, Amenhotep was Chief Designer in the Mansion's building department so such a project was mere child's play. About one fourth of the storehouse was separated from the rest by means of a false wall. With so much stacked inside it would have taken a very practised eye not to mention a measuring cord to notice that the volume didn't tally with the lengths of the external walls.'

'And how did one gain access to this cubbyhole?' the Prince asked.

'In one corner, apparently the back corner of the storeroom, a large and very old wooden chest stood against the wall. It was usually stacked about with jars and bundles and looked as if it hadn't been moved for years. But when the chest was lifted by means of the thick rope handles on either side, it brought away two planked boards which formed the floor beneath it and a section of the wall behind it. The boards were plastered over with mud, which was moulded to look like the brickwork of the storehouse itself, and this was so cunningly done that the cracks were invisible unless, of course, you knew what to look for. And beneath the chest was a narrow hole with three brick-built steps leading down and under the false wall. This brought you through to a sort of well in the corner of the inner store. You emerged with your chin at the level of the floor and it was dark but the smells told you at once that this was a real treasure house.'

Khaemwase nodded. He had been in enough storehouses to understand what the Count meant; that mixture of the heady perfumes of unguents, the sweet and aromatic scents of herbs and spices, the warm smell of leather and the sharp tang, almost taste, of metal. He had experienced the same assault on his senses in the temple repositories and in the tombs of his brothers and his mother where such valuables had been provided for the next life. Smell was such a powerful vehicle for the memory.

The Prince asked, 'Did Hatiay ever discover the existence of that store?'

'Not at the time, Highness, though we did show it to him before we left Waset. He never suspected that Simut had anything other than what could be seen in the main store. That, after all, was such a bizarre and bewildering sight that he could be forgiven for not looking further.
'

'And how did Simut go about explaining that bizarre and bewildering sight?'

'Largely with the help of Amenhotep's sons,' the Count said, then he lapsed into an uncharacteristic silence. Khaemwase and the Spy understood his feelings and both waited for him to regain his composure.

*

Each morning at the House of Life, the scribe school at the Temple of Amen-Ra, the students went to the gate court to collect their daily rations of bread and beer and any other supplies which their families could afford. Women brought the goods to the gate at dawn and as the sun rose, the doorkeeper slipped back the bolts and folded back the heavy wooden doors to allow them entry. The women who brought the supplies were mothers, sisters, household servants or one-time nurses of the youngsters who were resident students at the school. The morning ritual included the calling out of greetings and the exchange of gossip. Takhenet's problems had been high on the list of topics of conversation for many days. News of the appointment of a Royal Commission was the only talking point that morning, the day after Simut's return.

The student scribes came out into the gate court in many different ways. The youngest boys, some of them weeping, ran into the arms of their loved ones. The boys in the last three years of their basic training were harder and more self-assured. They adopted a supercilious swagger, though some were reticent about confronting their parents or sponsors if they knew their tutors had returned unfavourable reports. The oldest youths were those who were already specialising in a particular discipline. Among them was Haremheb, the second son of the Designer Amenhotep, who was surprised to find his elder brother Siamun waiting at the gate.

'You're needed at home today, Hari,' Siamun said, flinging an arm around his brother's shoulders. 'I've delivered Father's note to your tutor and you've got the day off. Officially! Let's make the most of it.'

Hari sensed in his brother's greeting that something was wrong. He knew instantly that it had to do with Takhenet's indiscretion which was already the talk of the school. He knew better than to ask awkward questions in such public surroundings so he said, 'A day off? That's just what I need!' and chatting and laughing, the two young men made their way through the Temple's administrative quarter and out of the main gateway.

The brothers were hardly more than a year apart in age but already Siamun's work as a stonemason had given him the muscular shoulders and upper arms of a much older man. People said he was very like his father's father, the old architect Ahmose, while Hari took after his mother's side of the family. Hari's hands were soft apart from the slight callus on the middle finger of his right hand which was permanently stained with ink. Siamun's large hands were rough and callused overall. The power of his grip was legendary in the dockside taverns where few cared to enter into a trial of strength with him. Despite these differences, Haremheb and Siamun were very close, closer even than Simut's twin sons Senusert and Nehesy.

At home the boys found their father and his brother waiting for them, both with serious, straight faces. They were ushered into

Amenhotep's workroom and the door was firmly closed. Not even Rai would have dared to disturb them.

Amenhotep indicated to the boys to sit down and then came straight to the point. 'You know that Takhenet has been accused of misappropriating royal stores. You must know that she is innocent. She has been foolish, certainly,' he nodded apologetically towards Simut, who bowed his head in acceptance, 'but she is not guilty of the charges brought against her. However, it is not as simple as that. If it were, we would not be talking to you now. There have been, and still are certain items in both our storerooms that would not bear a closer inspection by the Royal Commission which has been ordered.'

Siamun and Haremheb looked at each other in amazement. Siamun spoke first, 'Where does this stuff come from? Tomb robbery?'

'No,' Amenhotep flatly denied. 'We may not be entirely honest but we're not fools. I can't tell you any more than that, you'll have to take it on trust. This is a family secret and as yet we don't think you're ready to be told everything, but we need your help and your discretion if we are to get Takhenet out of this mess. Come with us to Simut's storehouse and we'll tell you what has to be done.'

Siamun and Hari were just as astounded by the contents of Simut's storehouse as their father and Hatiay had been. They were also impressed by the ingenuity of the hidden room.

'Is our storehouse made to the same design?' Siamun asked his father.

'Yes, son, though your mother doesn't know about it, any more than Takhenet knows about theirs, so mind your tongue. What we have to do is prevent any more attention being drawn to the family and protect the Secret. In her ignorance, Takhenet could cause untold damage. We cannot allow her to speak for herself in court. We'll have to speak for her. We'll have to cover our tracks and at the same time provide her with acceptable reasons for everything she's done.'

'Can we really do that?' Simut asked, sounding none too hopeful.

Amenhotep thought for a moment. 'It should be possible. What has she said to you already?'

'When I confronted her about all this,' Simut waved his hands vaguely about him indicating the piles of useless and wasted goods, 'she wept and raged and pleaded but she was still unrepentant. She thought that she was being a good housewife by accumulating all that stuff through bargaining and barter and scrimping and saving, when she had no need to. Even though half of it will never be of any use to anyone, she still tried to make it sound so sensible. She said she'd been preparing a dowry for Merytamen and then, of course, there are Nofret and Tiye to consider as they'll need dowries in time. And what about the funerals? The goods she's collected could be traded for tomb furniture and pay for a good coffin painter.... It just goes on and on. She honestly thought, when she went to the Temple stores, that she was entitled to the things she demanded. I couldn't convince her otherwise. She still thinks she's been perfectly rational and that everyone else is being unreasonable. It's like a sort of sickness, a sickness of the mind, and I have no idea how to cure her of it.'

Trying to divert his brother from more miserable thoughts, Amenhotep picked on something that Simut had said. 'That idea about accumulating dowry goods is not such a bad one, it would account for a good part of her stockpile. That could be the answer.'

'But Meryt isn't even betrothed yet,' Simut said.

Siamun nudged his brother in the ribs. Hari glared at him then spoke up. 'I've been meaning to speak to you about that.'

The two older men looked at Haremheb indulgently. They had always hoped that there might be at least one union of their children. Siamun seemed content to remain unmarried as long as possible but Hari and Meryt had been paired off at family parties since they were toddlers. Simut smiled, 'Thank you Hari, I had hoped to hear from you soon.'

Amenhotep embraced his son. 'Well done, boy. There's no rush for the wedding itself, Hari, but an official announcement of betrothal would be very timely.'

'And I suppose you want me to draw up some lists and invoices and so on to account for the dowry goods,' Haremheb said. Simut raised an eyebrow. Hari was as quick as Amenhotep had claimed.

'That's right, Hari,' his father said, 'we'll need as much documentation, cross-referenced and witnessed, as possible if we're to stand a chance of blinkering the court. If you draught the documents we can spread them around the city with various other scribes to make copies for the court's use.'

Hari grinned, 'Then we swap around the originals and the copies so that the invoices and receipts are all in different handwriting while the set for the court is all in my hand. After all, who else would you trust to prepare the trial documents?'

'Exactly,' Amenhotep beamed and turned to Simut. 'You see, Simy, the plan is workable and with Hari's help we can make it work. As for you, Siamun, you can help me with the inventory. We can't do much about Simut's stores but there's some dead wood we can clear from our own. We've got to rationalise. They haven't got around to searching our premises yet but it's only a matter of time. Once the royal seals go on the doors we won't have a chance.'

'When does the court convene?' Siamun asked, meaning, 'How long have we got?'

'Whenever His Highness arrives in Waset and that could be any day now, depending on how keen he is to get on with the case.'

'So we'd better get started, hadn't we?' Siamun grinned, trying to look and sound more cheerful than he felt.

The next two days were rest days for most royal employees but in the privacy of their family storerooms Amenhotep and his sons worked harder than ever. When they came to appreciate the size and value of the collection of goods gathered together by Takhenet, the boys were stunned.

'What a waste,' Siamun muttered.

Hari mused, 'It would have been a generous dowry if it was all new.'

'We can't touch any of this,' their father warned. 'Remember, Hatiay has a full inventory. Simut has to keep scrupulous account of anything in the way of foodstuffs removed from here before the case comes to court. Apart from that, he mustn't move anything.'

Hari ran his hand over the topmost sheet in a pile of bed linen. 'What's the current value of a linen sheet?' he asked, 'and has it changed much in recent years?' His gaze fell to the mouldering cloth at the bottom of the pile. Amenhotep grunted, 'We'll have to find out a lot about relative values if we're to explain away things like that.'

'Yes, and the longer the period of time we can prove that it took to gather all this stuff together, the more realistic our case will look,' Hari said. 'I'll have to draw up invoices back-dated as far as possible. It'll take time.'

'We haven't got much time,' his father said. 'I'm afraid it's a race between us and the Prince's boat and we don't even know when the race started.'

‘Then I’d better get going,’ Hari said as he began to set out his writing equipment on a pile of reed mats. He was soon hard at work drawing up lists of items which he estimated to be of the same age. His delicate hand moved quickly over the scroll and in his concentration his tongue poked slightly from between his teeth.

Siamun, looking over his brother’s shoulder at the list he was compiling, said, ‘If I count and call out the items you want, will that speed things up?’

Hari smiled his thanks and Amenhotep left his sons working together. He had to talk with Simut about the announcement of the betrothal. He wondered how Merytamen had taken the news.

*

At about the same time, Sunero had arrived in Waset and his preliminary report for the Prince was the next document to be drawn from the box.

The Scribe Sunero greets his Lord, the most High Prince Khaemwase. Bearing Your Lordship’s commission, I have presented myself to Mahu, Deputy to Your Highness’s kinsman, the Lord Tjia, at the King’s Mansion Temple. I find him, as your Lordship predicted, incredulous that any irregularity may be found in the running of the Mansion of His Majesty. He is unwilling to probe too deeply into the case himself for fear of the Lord Tjia’s reaction to what might be seen as a test of his competency. Lord Tjia is already most resentful that the Crown Prince has been drawn into his affairs, and his staff, Mahu in particular, are all suffering from his uncharacteristically sharp tongue and his unusually short temper. I have not dared to approach him myself. Even if I could fight my way beyond Mahu’s office, the Lord Tjia’s own personal staff are known to be very protective of their Lord. It would be expense of effort to no purpose.

I have had private conversation with Senmut, the secretary of the Tjaty Paser, and have found him to be efficient and well-informed as to the situation here. However, he confirms that the Tjaty sees no reason to involve the Crown Prince in what he calls ‘this little local difficulty’. I fear the Tjaty himself has effectively dismissed the affair as being beneath his notice and, clearly, Lord Tjia is of much the same opinion. Both will wish to be rid of this annoying interruption to the smooth running of their departments. With the Jubilee preparations well under way, neither feels he has the time to deal with a petty official’s complaint.

If it were not for the Scribe Hatiay's unshakeable belief that something is very seriously amiss here in Waset, I too would recommend that the case is not worth pursuing. As it is, I have enquired among the wives of the Temple employees. Their animosity towards the accused woman, Takhenet, seems to be based almost entirely on envy. She is, I am told, a woman of haughty demeanour and over-proud, which will not endear her to many of her kind. But the real complaint against her is that she seems to be better provided for than the wives of employees who are of similar rank to her husband, Simut. The difference in the standard of living would not be so remarkable if Takhenet did not boast of her riches. I have not been able to ascertain the value of the dowry which she brought to the marriage, but I do not think that she came from a particularly wealthy family.

As to her husband, Simut, the Scribe Accountant of the Temple Herds, he has but recently returned from preparing a census in the Northern Realm. He is of good family being the second son of the Architect Ahmose. He is very close to his brother, the Chief Designer in the Building Department of the Mansion, who also lives a comfortable existence, perhaps exceptionally comfortable in the circumstances. No one has a bad word to say against either Simut or his brother, Amenhotep. They are model servants of His Majesty, carrying out their duties without the slightest hint of disloyalty or dissatisfaction. I have found not one shred of evidence that either Simut or his brother might even contemplate an illegal act. The very suggestion brings disbelieving laughter to the lips of anyone who hears it. The woman Takhenet may be despised and derided but her husband and his brother are seen as beyond reproach. It is the spotless reputation of these two men that gives me to believe that the Scribe Hatiay has chanced upon a matter of a serious nature, for no family is so perfect, no man can be so unequivocally virtuous.

As Your Lordship has ordered, I continue to pursue the matter, for I become more convinced by the day that His Majesty may be the victim of a most cunning plot.

One day out from Waset, the boat bearing Sunero's letter to his master had to give way to the royal barge bringing Crown Prince Ramesses to the Southern City. The following morning at the Western Town quay, the royal barge docked and the Prince stepped ashore to the cheers of the local garrison troops. Like his father, Ramesses was a tall man with broad shoulders and striking features. As was his custom, he wore the simple kilt and lightweight shirt of a soldier but elaborated this costume with a wide collar inlaid with multi-coloured glass. Heavy gold armbands worn above the elbow and a gaudy beaded belt with an apron front which clanked with plates of gold and bronze completed his outfit. To keep his large hands occupied he held a small ceremonial axe, awarded to him for his part in the Battle of Kadesh. This was a very minor part, since the Prince had not reached his teens at the time, but no one would dare to make that point. His figure and appearance were impressive, his carriage imposing, but his eyes were vacant. There was no spark of intelligence, nor the least suggestion that an original thought might ever have blossomed in the royal consciousness.

With a wave of the axe the Prince indicated that Hanufer, the Mayor of Waset, should rise from his obeisance and then went forward to grasp the outstretched hand of his father's old friend and his own one-time tutor Paser, the Tjaty of the South.

'Long life, prosperity and health to Your Royal Highness,' Paser spoke the formal greeting softly in a voice that commanded immediate respect from the listener.

'Good to see you again,' Ramesses bellowed. He had never mastered the art of conversation. He addressed everyone, high and low alike, as if he were drilling them on the parade ground. 'D'you know what all this is about? Has Sethi told you anything? Can't say I know what I'm doing here, damned if I can.'

Paser shook his head very slightly and by a faint frown indicated that now was not the time, nor here the place for discussion. The welcoming party tactfully directed the royal visitor to the waiting chariots and within moments he was racing along the causeway towards his father's great Mansion temple.

Having been installed in his apartments in the small royal residence adjoining the temple, the Prince went to pay his respects to the widowed husband of his father's sister, the Lord Tjia.

Ramesses had hoped for a quiet family meeting, a few jars of beer and a good meal. Lord Tjia had a reputation for keeping the finest table in Waset. Instead, the Prince found the Superintendent of the Mansion in his reception hall surrounded by a small battalion of bureaucrats, the very sort of person that made Ramesses most uncomfortable. The clerks being mar-shalled by the Mansion Deputy, Mahu, were apparently up to their armpits in bundles of papyrus scrolls and boxes of the limestone fragments on which memoranda were recorded. It was clear that Lord Tjia intended to get down to business straight away. Ramesses felt the beginnings of a headache behind his left ear at the very thought of the tedium that awaited him.

Watching as Hatiay and Riya were called forward to explain themselves to the assembled dignitaries, Sunero stood in the shadows of the colonnade, holding himself aloof from the local officials. While the scribe and the store-keeper retold, in the simplest terms, the events which had resulted in the ordering of a royal inquiry, Sunero watched faces. Lord Tjia looked annoyed and Mahu harassed. Paser might have appeared bored, but those, like Sunero, who knew the wily politician of old, recognised that his air of quiet disdain had been cultivated over thirty years as the King's Tjaty in the South to maintain a disinterested front. Those eyes took in every nuance of appearance and those ears heard every word. Takhenet was lucky that Paser had more pressing matters of state to concern him so that he would not be taking part personally in her trial.

Sunero's appraising eye next fell on Prince Ramesses whose face remained totally blank. There was no way of telling whether he had taken in anything of what had been said. Sunero privately thought that if the Prince understood one word in three of what he had heard it could be considered a miracle. Once the preliminary facts had been established, Hatiay and Riya were questioned closely but neither could be shaken from his belief that they had acted only in the King's interest. Sunero studied Hatiay closely. While the lords discussed the matter between themselves, the scribe was biting his nails with aggravation. Sunero recognised an intelligent man trapped in a job which was beneath his capabilities. Hatiay knew or suspected more than could be properly said. He was a man worth talking to in private.

Lord Tjia rapped on the floor with his walking staff. The room fell silent. 'I have heard enough,' he said, his voice quavering with age and indignation. 'I will bear the aspersions cast upon my management of the King's Mansion because it seems that these two servants truly believe their case to be valid. I, of course, do not share that belief. However genuinely they believed, I cannot see that it was necessary to impose upon the time of either of our exalted Tjatys, much less to involve His Royal Highness in such a paltry and essentially local matter. But, whatever my own views might be, a Royal Inquiry has been ordered and His Royal Highness is here. The system must be allowed to run its usual course. My only wish is that it should be dealt with as quickly as possible so that His Highness might not be kept unnecessarily long from his other duties.'

Prince Ramesses' nod gave the first sign that he had listened to and understood anything. Lord Tjia continued, 'I think our next step is to convene the court. Let warrants be issued for the detention of this woman...' he referred to his notes, '...er, yes, Takhenet, and for the presentation of all the evidence, if there is any to be found. It is so ordered.' With that cutting comment Lord Tjia rapped the staff on the floor again to indicate that the preliminary hearing was over. The lesser officials bowed or abased themselves as the Superintendent of the Mansion escorted the Crown Prince from the hall. Prince Ramesses was heard to sigh with relief and his spirits seemed to have been revived by the thought of the meal awaiting him in Lord Tjia's private quarters. The Tjaty and the Mayor led their retinues back towards their own offices allowing the remaining clerks to debate the correct procedure for drawing up the necessary warrants. Sunero moved closer so that he could overhear their discussions.

He immediately saw that Hatiay's opinion and judgement were far more highly regarded by his peers than by his superiors. The Scribe Accountant was asked what warrants he required and the clerks were prepared to word the documents in whatever way Hatiay dictated. This, Sunero thought, was how Hatiay had managed to have his fears voiced as far away as Mennefer. There was a conspiracy of support amongst the Mansion employees for one of their own who was well respected and trusted, and Sunero guessed that there were few in Hatiay's position who could have claimed such loyalty.

The documents were quickly prepared; an arrest warrant for Takhenet and an order for the sealing of Simut's storerooms would be enacted at dawn the following day. At the same time, a summons to attend the court, including full details of the charges to be brought against the woman, was to be delivered to her husband together with a demand that he should make available all relevant documents that might be required in evidence. Finally, a public notice was drafted to the effect that the case against Takhenet would be heard in the Mansion Court beginning on the day after the issue of the summons.

Sunero was impressed. Hatiay had arranged everything neatly and efficiently without overburdening the clerks. He had thought of everything except for those matters which were beyond his influence. As to that, Sunero needed to talk to Hatiay quickly. With practised skill the Spy caught the Scribe by the arm as he was about to leave and drew him into the furthest recess of the colonnade. Hatiay hardly had time to protest before Sunero, in a low urgent voice, was speaking his piece. Even in the shadows, the expression on Hatiay's face could be seen to change from indignation through surprise to quiet satisfaction.

He grasped Sunero's hand. 'Thank you,' he said. It was enough to know that, whatever the outcome of the court case, someone believed him, some one took him seriously.

By order of the Superintendent of the Mansion of His Majesty, the Lord Tjia. The woman, Takhenet, wife of the Scribe Accountant of the Herds of Amen-Ra, Simut, is to be detained pending her appearance before the court of inquiry. This warrant to be enacted by the Medjay Mermose and two security officers. Anyone hindering Mermose in the enactment of his duty will suffer the penalty set down for obstructing justice. So ordered by the Lord Tjia, under his seal.

By order of the Superintendent of the Mansion of His Majesty, the Lord Tjia. The storerooms belonging to the Scribe Accountant of the Herds of Amen-Ra, Simut, are hereby sealed pending the trial of the said Simut's wife, Takhenet. Let no one break the seals upon the doors of these storerooms on penalty of being charged with obstructing justice. So ordered by the Lord Tjia, under his seal.

By order of the Superintendent of the Mansion of His Majesty, the Lord Tjia. Be it known that the Scribe Accountant of the Herds of Amen-Ra, Simut, is summoned to appear at the Mansion Court to account for the actions of his wife, the woman Takhenet. He is informed hereby of the charges laid against his wife;

Firstly, that she did, in haughty manner, demand supplies from the royal stores which were not hers to demand.

Secondly, that she defied the authority of the Overseer of the Royal Stores, Riya, and did by her words cause him insult.

Thirdly, that by her own admission she has, on many occasions, claimed goods from the royal stores to which she was not entitled.

Fourthly, that she had hoarded certain goods, within the storerooms of her husband, that may be proved to have come from the royal stores.

Fifthly, that the woman, Takhenet, has, over an undetermined period of time, consistently misappropriated royal stores and has, by means of fraudulent conversion, been supporting her family at the expense of His Majesty.

The Scribe Accountant of the Herds of Amen-Ra, Simut, is hereby commanded to release into the hands of the Scribe Accountant, Hatiay, any and all documents which may be demanded of him as being relevant to this case. Nothing shall be withheld on pain of suffering the penalty for obstructing justice. So ordered by the Lord Tjia, under his seal.

Be it known that the woman Takhenet, wife of the Scribe Accountant of the Herds of Amen-Ra, Simut, has been detained by the Medjay of the Mansion of His Majesty. The woman, Takhenet, is to be brought before the royal court of inquiry on the day following this day, there to answer the charges brought against her. By order of the Lord Tjia, Superintendent of the Mansion of His Majesty.

*

'So, the fat was well and truly smoking,' said Khaemwase with a certain smugness in his voice. 'I can plainly imagine my dear brother's reaction and your description of Lord Tjia was perfect, just perfect. It all seems so real, so recent. If only the years could be rolled away so easily. Twenty-five years, half a lifetime for most people.'

'Twenty-five years is nothing in a long-lived family like Your Highness's,' the Count was quick to remark.

'Some of us live longer than is seemly,' the Prince said under his breath but not so quietly that Sunero could not hear him. The Spy groaned inwardly. For a moment he had thought they had won, that they had restored Khaemwase's enthusiasm for life, but the Count's retort had undone all the good of the last few hours. He had meant to be encouraging, Sunero realised, but he could not read the Prince's mood as the Spy had learnt to do over his years in Khaemwase's service. Any reminder of the King's apparent immortality was painful to his son.

Khaemwase waved his hand in a gesture of dismissal, 'Go now, home to your families. Tomorrow is another day.'

They could do nothing except bow themselves out. In the anteroom Sunero rounded on his friend, 'Your mouth runs away with you too often. Do you know what you've done?'

'Made him think?' the Count said lightly.

'Think, yes, but about all the wrong things. You've reminded him that the King, gods preserve him, is still alive and kicking. That's the very reason he's become as depressed as he is. He has no prospects. He sees no future for himself. At least while we keep him in the past he has something to look forward to.'

'He'll not give up yet. He wants to hear everything.'

'But how long will this story take? Just how much can we stretch it out?'

'You're overreacting, Sunero,' the Count scoffed. 'He's hooked. We can play him like a fish, land him when we want and then throw him back. He'll live. He's too stubborn to give in now.'

Sunero shrugged, a helpless gesture. What other hope was there?

Chapter Four

Next morning, when Sunero and the Count presented themselves at the lodge of the Prince's residence, they were surprised to find that the gatekeeper had orders to admit them only to the garden. 'You're to wait there until you're sent for. On no account am I to let you into the house and on no account am I to let you leave the premises.'

They were too bemused to argue. For some while they wandered in silence around the ornamental pond and between the vine trellises. At last the Count said, 'It's a good sign.'

'How can you possibly think that?'

'He's annoyed with us, with me in particular. He's making us wait as a form of punishment.'

'But isn't that punishing himself too? Have you considered that he might be too ill to see us? That he might have faded overnight?'

'No. If he was really ill the gatekeeper would have known and there'd be so much fuss going on that we'd have been forgotten. The Prince gave the orders himself. He's punishing us, that's what it is.'

There was just so much they could do in the garden before boredom set in. They tried skimming stones over the pool but the water lilies spread so widely that the only clear surface area allowed two skips at most. Then they ran out of stones since Khaemwase's efficient gardeners kept the beds raked and the paths swept. A side trip to the vegetable plot gave them an opportunity for conversation with a monosyllabic and apparently simple gardener who was watering the leeks. They watched as he went to and fro, carrying heavy jars on a yoke across his shoulders, filling them at the cistern and emptying them over the rows of thirsty plants. Some time was spent in their failed attempts to get him to talk about anything other than his vegetables. They were more successful in persuading him to share some of the homemade wine of which he was so proud. He had a small skin of it hanging in the shady branches of an acacia tree. Sunero's first gulp nearly knocked him flat. He tried to hide his reaction to the mouth-wrenchingly dry liquor as he handed the skin to his friend. The Count's eyes almost came out on stalks as the wine hit the back of his throat. It was some while before either man could speak. Meanwhile the gardener wandered away almost doubled over with helpless giggling.

'He's easily amused,' the Count said at last, wiping his eyes.

'His throat must be lined with granite,' Sunero croaked. 'What is that stuff made of?'

'I'd guess it's got nothing to do with grapes. Sycomore fruit I shouldn't wonder. By the gods it's strong!'

With the same thought, the two men went to the tank and scooped up handfuls of water to dilute the gardener's evil brew. They were sitting on the cistern's edge when the Prince's servant, Userhet, found them. 'His Highness commands your presence now,' the man said, looking down his long nose at their dishevelled appearance.

'How is His Highness this morning?' Sunero asked as he ran his fingers through his short wavy hair. He was well known to all Khaemwase's household servants and had personally approved this man's appointment.

'It's not my place to comment,' Userhet said stiffly before looking around quickly to be sure he was not overheard, 'but I'd be pretty careful in choosing my words, if I were you. I don't think he slept and I know Master Montmose is still very worried about him.'

'Montmose is always worrying about something. It's his job to worry,' the Count said, brushing dust from his kilt.

'But some give him more cause to worry than others,' Userhet said, with a pointed look in the Count's direction, 'and Montmose's worries affect the whole household. We'd be grateful if you could give him something to be cheerful about.'

'Any suggestions?' the Count asked with a twinkling smile.

'The news that you were about to leave the country and never come back,' the servant said with a perfectly straight face.

'Not just yet,' the Count laughed, 'Sorry to disappoint you.'

'Let's stop playing games and remember why we're here,' Sunero snapped. The Count shrugged and Userhet turned on his heel to lead them back into the house.

Khaemwase was leaning back in a cushioned armchair on the dais in the anteroom, his feet resting on a leather-covered footstool. At his side was a fruit bowl on a stand and a wine jar fitted with a siphon. The Prince's butler hovered behind his master, awaiting the order to serve his guests. Khaemwase held out a golden goblet to be filled but indicated that Sunero and the Count should sit on the little wooden stools which had been placed in front of the dais with the file box between them. They were not offered wine and the butler was dismissed. The two friends waited as the Prince sipped his drink watching them intently all the while over the rim of his cup. At last he lowered the goblet to rest on the arm of his chair saying, 'So, you have returned. Well, get on with the story. My time is limited.'

Sunero spared a quick glance at his companion. The Count seemed to be unmoved and unworried. He took up the tale as if the interruption had been for but a few moments.

*

When the Medjay, Mermose, arrived at Simut's door with two burly attendants, Takhenet had hysterics. Simut had his eldest daughter, Merytamen, take charge of her mother while he dealt with the formalities. He had hoped that his wife would be confined under house arrest in his care until the trial but one glance at the warrant in Mermose's pudgy hand disabused him of that idea. A protest would only result in worse trouble. Mermose was not one to put up with any nonsense. He had his orders and he was going to carry them out to the least detail. As Takhenet was taken from the arms of her weeping daughter, Simut stood to one side, helpless. Merytamen turned to be comforted by her betrothed, the scribe Haremheb, as her mother was dragged away screaming from the house. In parting, Mermose handed Simut a copy of the charge document including the demand to submit the relevant papers to the court. 'As soon as you can,' the Medjay said tersely.

Simut stood, with misery written all over his face, as Takhenet was carried away bodily to the quay where she was to be put on a boat and taken across the river to the guardhouse at the Mansion. Her cries of, 'Simy! Simy! Don't let them take me! Simy, please!' echoed along the street bringing curious neighbours to their doors to watch and speculate in low voices. Simut could stand it no more. He withdrew into his house and bolted the door behind him.

By creeping out of the servants' entrance and clambering in a most undignified way over the low walls around the animal pens, Simut and Haremheb made their way to Amenhotep's home to prepare their case for the Crown Prince's court on the following day. The documents which Hari had drawn up were really quite impressive. By strategic placing of copying work with a number of different scribes on both sides of the River, and by providing them with a variety of materials including worn and reused papyrus, scraps of leather and limestone flakes, a convincing collection of invoices, bills of sale and deeds of gift had been accumulated. These were added to the records which

Simut himself had kept of major purchases and exchanges. Hari's originals together with his neat copy of Simut's archive were filed in a leather document case acquired specially for the occasion. This was to be presented to the court as a rationalisation of all the documents which would, of course, be available on request for inspection.

Included in the file case was a new, crisp, clean scroll detailing the transfer of goods and property pertaining to Hari's betrothal to Meryt. The family hoped that this would be Takhenet's prime line of defence. Who could condemn a mother for wishing to provide her daughter with the best possible start to her married life? They hoped to prove that Takhenet had started to collect this dowry even when Meryt was only a few months old and that she had no idea how certain goods would deteriorate over the years. There was also a poignant group of genuine documents which told of the funeral arranged for Takhenet's youngest son, Khuy. The boy had been born early and had never thrived. The fact that he had lived to be nearly three years old was testament to the care and devotion Takhenet had lavished on her lastborn. Payments for the child's coffin and a painted linen shroud were detailed and from this it was clear that, as far as Takhenet was concerned, nothing was too good for her children. There was more than a little truth in the case which Amenhotep and Simut were preparing. Takhenet had been devastated by Khuy's death. They hoped that her volatile emotional state could excuse many of her irrational actions.

Haremheb was nominated as the family's scribe to keep a private record of the court's proceedings. Simut and Amenhotep were to speak for Takhenet. Siamun was told to go to work as usual to prevent drawing too much attention to the rest of the family.

Sunero had been admitted to the court as an observer but kept himself well out of the way, determined that he should not overstep his authority. The courtroom was a forbidding place. The judges sat on chairs each varying in quality according to the rank of its occupant. In the centre sat Crown Prince Ramesses in a gilded armchair with a cow-hide seat and a cushion for his back. The senior local judge was Mahu, the Deputy of the Mansion, who sat on the Prince's right while to the left was Djehuti who represented the Tjaty Paser. Their armless chairs were inlaid with ivory while those of the two lesser judges, Ramose from the Finance Department and Penabdu from the Treasury, were of plain wood with woven rush seats. The recording scribes sat cross-legged on the floor in front of the dais and to one side was the brick-built bench on which the documents were to be displayed by the Clerk of the Court.

The brothers and Haremheb had been ushered in to take their places on the floor to the left of the platform. To the right were Takhenet's accusers, Hatiay and Riya, with their scribes. The last person to enter the courtroom was the accused, Takhenet, who was almost carried in by two Medjay guards. Her face was stained with tears and dark shadows beneath her eyes testified to a sleepless night. She was forced to kneel and then touch her forehead to the floor in the Prince's presence. Because her arms were tied behind her back in the manner prescribed for criminals she could not lift herself up again and had to be helped with little gentleness by one of the guards. Simut groaned and swallowed a sob. Takhenet's eyes were vacant. Her husband recognised the signs. He knew she had retreated into herself as she had done after Khuy's death. He doubted that she would recover this time.

Sunero studied the faces of the judges. Crown Prince Ramesses wore a permanent frown of aggravation. Mahu was surveying the people before him with a somewhat supercilious gaze while Djehuti seemed to be nursing a hangover. Ramose and Penabdu looked rather bewildered to find themselves in such exalted company. They had had little time to absorb any but the main facts of the case they were about to hear and neither understood what was going on. Turning his attention to the main body of the hall, Sunero noted with satisfaction the calm look on Hatiay's face. Their conversation had been mutually reassuring and Hatiay knew that, win or lose, he had not been wrong in bringing his suspicions into the open. In the faces of the brothers Simut and Amenhotep he read both despair and hope. Simut could not bring himself to look in his wife's direction. He sat on the floor with his chin resting on his chest. Amenhotep looked alert. He was facing the court boldly and with an air of confidence that owed much to the fine job done by his son in preparing the bundle of documents.

After a respectful reminder from Mahu, the Crown Prince brought the court to order and had the Clerk read out the charges. In that dreary hall with its oppressive shadows and the temperature rising as the sun mounted higher and bodies sweated, the charges against Takhenet sounded pitifully vague and almost impossible to prove. Prince Ramesses now knew what everyone else had long suspected.

This case was a waste of time. The sooner it was over the better for all concerned. He banged his great fist down on the arm of his chair.

'I haven't got all day. This hearing will be finished by midday, that is my order. I don't want any waffling or dissembling. I want to hear the straight facts with no embroidery and I will come to a decision which will be final, with no right of appeal. I hope I make myself clear. Now, I will decide who will speak and in what order.' He turned to consult Mahu who checked with the scroll containing the names of all those concerned in the case and whispered a name. 'Yes,' Prince Ramesses said in his usual loud voice, 'I call on the Overseer of the Royal Stores, Riya. You're the one who first had cause to complain about the woman. Let's have your story, and keep it short.'

Sunero sighed as Riya bowed to the judges and began his deposition. Hatiay was going to lose the case. The Prince's overturning of all the usual court procedures and the time limit he had imposed would make Hatiay's position untenable. Ramesses cut Riya's self-important speech short with an impatient wave of his axe, saying, 'Enough. I don't need to know everything the woman said to you. I get the idea. She was rude and you felt insulted. Fair enough. She should have known her place. I find her guilty of that charge.'

The Tjaty's representative Djehuti made as if to question this judgement but one look at the Prince's scowling face rapidly changed his mind. He sagged in his chair with a resigned expression which said clearly, 'The Prince has spoken and I'm not brave enough to argue with a prince.'

Ramesses, heartened by this success, said, 'Now, I want to hear from the storekeeper who first dealt with the woman. Let's find out just what she wanted from the warehouses.'

Sunero was surprised. Prince Ramesses was showing signs of a hitherto unsuspected intelligence. Then the Spy had an inspiration. The Prince had been coached by Lord Tjia. Ramesses was repeating his lesson well, albeit in his own words rather than the more measured phrases the elderly nobleman would have used. Sunero nodded his head in appreciation. Lord Tjia had learnt his craft as an administrator and manager under the previous king, the God Sethy, whose daughter he had married. Though long ago widowed, his talents, allied with stalwart support for the kingship of his wife's brother, had kept him close to the royal family. His appointment, early in the reign, as Superintendent of the King's new Mansion Temple, had come as no surprise. The old man was still a wily bird, with many years of experience behind him. The King had the utmost faith in his sister's husband, calling him his brother and recommending Lord Tjia's wisdom to his own sons.

With no children of his own surviving, Lord Tjia had been glad and honoured to take on the role of father to the young princes whenever they were resident in Waset. Crown Prince Ramesses in particular was very much in awe of Lord Tjia's authority and would have been only too glad to accept his advice in the conduct of this case. The Superintendent's initial indignation at the suggestion of any maladministration on his part had so matched Ramesses' resentful attitude that the two had been able to plan a campaign which the Prince, as a military man, could easily visualise and understand. They would deal with each charge by taking the line of least resistance. Takhenet would be found guilty of excessive demands on the royal stores as well as challenging Riya's authority, but the other charges would be unprovable and would be dismissed. One look at Hatiay told Sunero that the Scribe had reached the same conclusion. The whole pointless exercise might just as well be abandoned. It was a mockery.

The storekeeper had mumbled his way through the list of goods which Takhenet had demanded. Ramesses was growing impatient again.

'Enough! Even to me it is clear that she was asking for goods to which she was not entitled.' Sunero grinned at the words which must have been dictated by Lord Tjia. The Prince continued, 'Overbearing, demanding, insolent. This is not a pretty picture. It is time we heard from the woman's husband. Stand up Simut.'

The miserable Simut rose slowly to his feet and bowed double before the judges. Ramesses waved his axe in the general direction of the hall. 'Stand up, man! Let's get on with it. The sun is getting ever closer to its height. Tell the court about that storeroom of yours. Tell us about how your wife managed to fill it with all that stuff.'

Simut lifted his head and a shudder ran through him as he took a deep breath and began his prepared explanation. At Haremheb's insistence he had cut the statement down to its bare bones. 'Simple words from a simple man, that's what the court will understand,' his brother's son had said. 'Make them feel sympathy for you but do it in as few words as absolutely necessary.' They had rehearsed the speech until Simut could have recited it in his sleep. He looked almost as if he was sleep-walking at that moment. At appropriate points in the speech

Hari handed relevant documents to the Clerk for comparison with the papyri which had been lodged with the court earlier. Sunero had to admire the slick preparation of this case. Simut was the perfect portrait of the troubled husband of an acquisitive wife. He had done his best to provide for her but she had always wanted more. By the time he came to describe her habit of hoarding unnecessary goods, most of those assembled in the court were feeling sorry for him. At the description of her reaction to Khuy's death one of the scribes sniffed loudly and wiped his nose with the back of his hand. The vivid picture Simut painted of the mouldering, useless goods which Takhenet had been accumulating for her daughter's dowry had even the hardened finance officer surreptitiously wiping an eye. Sunero was impressed. It was a masterly display and totally convincing, but it only served to confirm his belief that Simut was far from being the blameless man that everyone thought him to be.

Finally, Simut raised his hands, palms upward in a beseeching gesture.

'I beg His Highness and the dignitaries here gathered to believe me. I swear by all the gods that nothing in my storerooms has been taken illegally or by deception from the royal stores of the Mansion. I here declare that if anything be found in my possession that shall be proved to have come from the royal stores other than by way of legitimate payment, then I shall repay it twofold. Should any of the goods which the Scribe Hatiay has declared to be missing from the royal stores be found amongst my goods then let them be brought to the Court this very day. I say that any such deficit is likely to be attributable to the guardians of the royal stores who are seeking to transfer their guilt to me. It is they who should be investigated in this court. The envious, wagging tongues of their wives have brought this evil upon us and have caused my wife such pain. See her now! She is a broken woman. Let me take her home. What purpose can be served by persecuting such as her?'

Simut let his arms fall to his sides. There was a long pause before the Prince cleared his throat and absently handed the last of the papyrus sheets back to the Clerk of the Court. He had hardly glanced at any of Hari's neat work over which the young scribe had taken such pains, but the very fact of the documents' being there, punctuating Simut's affecting monologue, had added both weight and poignancy to his words. Hatiay was resting his head in his hands. He knew he had lost, for now.

From the moment the Crown Prince began his summing up it was clear that the case had been tried and the outcome decided in the privacy of the Superintendent's residence. Ramesses' words, though less formal than those Lord Tjia would have used, conveyed the sentiments of the official opinion already expressed and the sentence handed down was that which had been agreed in advance of the trial. Ramesses said at last, 'I understand how easy it is for one person to arouse the envy of others through no fault of their own. I have seen it in the army...'

'And in his own family,' Khaemwase interjected.

'...No proof of misappropriation or fraud has been presented. I have seen only the sad evidence of a woman who has earned the jealousy and contempt of her fellows. I have neither seen nor heard anything that convinces me that this pitiful woman is a thief, certainly not on the scale suggested by the charges. Although she has overstepped the mark in a couple of areas I think her husband can be trusted to see that this does not happen again. So, I will release her into the custody of her husband, Simut, on the understanding that he will swear to keep his wife under strict control. He is also to pay to the court an amount in goods by way of a fine, equivalent to...' he looked towards the Treasury officer who nodded eagerly. 'Oh, that can be sorted out later. That, I think, is all that need be said of the matter. I declare this Court dismissed.'

And that was that. Ramesses stood. The noise of his chair being pushed back echoed through the stunned courtroom. Belatedly, everybody bowed to the floor as the judges followed the Prince out of the room. Then Amenhotep embraced his brother while Hatiay, already resigned to the inevitability of defeat, patted Riya's back in consolation. The guards cut Takhenet's bonds and dragged her to hand her over to her husband. Sunero had seen enough. He had a report to write.

*

Khaemwase sighed, 'Ah, yes. That report. I believe that was the one I never saw.'

'Yes, Sir. By the time I despatched it to the North, Your Highness had already set off on the Jubilee tour.'

'Yes, I had quite a few important things on my mind, as I recall. The Jubilee had to be proclaimed in the major cities, the gods informed and invited to the celebrations in Mennefer, and the Apis was dying. That, in particular, was not an auspicious start to the King's first Jubilee. I hated having to leave Mennefer at such a time. Your little bit of bother in Waset was very low down on my list of priorities.'

'In Waset, Your Highness, it was all that we talked about,' the Count said.

'I can well believe it. It never ceases to amaze me how petty-minded even the Holy City can be. So tell me, Sunero, without reading out the whole report, which I'm sure you have to hand, what happened after my brother had dispensed his form of justice.'

*

While Sunero had been compiling his report in the tiny office allocated to him by Lord Tjia's Deputy, Hatiay was receiving a severe reprimand from the same Mahu. Riya had already expressed his feelings in no uncertain terms, accusing Hatiay of leading him by the nose into this fiasco of a trial in which the Overseer of the Royal Stores had been made to look ridiculous. Riya had no trouble in convincing himself that Hatiay alone was to blame for his loss of face and the bad impression he was sure he had made on the Crown Prince. Hatiay was perfectly well aware that his own reputation and career were to be sacrificed to appease the hurt feelings of all those who considered they had suffered because of the case brought against Takhenet. He took his dressing-down calmly, hardly hearing what the Deputy of the Mansion was saying. Finally, emerging from Mahu's presence, he should have been thoroughly depressed and demoralised. Anyone who saw his jaunty walk across the compound to keep his appointment with Sunero would never have guessed that Hatiay had just been demoted to the rank of ordinary clerk. He knocked boldly at Sunero's door.

'Come in, Hatiay.' The scribe was surprised to be called by name, but within a few months of their association, his familiarity with Sunero's working practices enabled him to appreciate the powers of deduction and observation that enabled the Spy, apparently, to see through a solid wooden door. Sunero turned from his writing and put down his pen. 'Come in and sit down. It went much as we expected, I'd say, except it was all over a lot more quickly than anyone could have predicted. You're not disappointed, arc you?'

'Not as much as I might have been, though I have lost my job.'

Sunero smiled, 'We expected that too, didn't we? But my offer still holds. His Highness, Prince Khaemwase, needs an agent in Waset.

He has properties in and around the Holy City and he needs a local man to look after his concerns. Are you still interested?'

'What do you think?'

'Good. I'll recommend your appointment to His Highness. You are Khaemwase's man from now on. Meanwhile, let's try to unravel this tangle. Let's see if we can't find out where the thread was knotted. Knowledge is the key. We must know what they know or we can never beat them.'

For the remainder of the daylight hours and into the darkness, the two men went over every fine detail of the court case. They discussed the Crown Prince's attitude and Hatiay was glad to hear that his new employer, Prince Khaemwase, was not to be compared with his royal brother. They dissected Simut's speech sentence by sentence until they were able to see how it had been constructed to have the greatest effect on his listeners. More and more they became convinced that Simut was the most cunning of men and that he had, to support him, the most remarkable of families.

'But we shall have them one day, Hatiay. I am determined that we shall have them!'

*

'And did you "have them"?' Khaemwase asked, though he already knew the answer.

'Not immediately, Sir, and not completely, but the chase was a good one.'

'So I remember. Now, Count, tell me your side of things.'

*

The homecoming of Takhenet was not as triumphant as the family had hoped. She was in a state of emotional and physical collapse. The one night she had spent in the Mansion's guardhouse had not been so terrible. Mermose's wife had taken pity on her and had provided her with decent food and had seen to it that she had water, towels and a comb to tidy herself up for her court appearance. But Takhenet's spirit had been broken. She could not face the indignity of appearing as a common criminal. Before her own kind it would have been bad enough. Before the officials of the Mansion and the Tjaty's court, the sort of people she would like to emulate, it was humiliating. But before the Crown Prince, second only to the King himself, her shame was total and it had consumed her spirit. Any plans for a celebration were set aside 'until Takhenet feels better.' But she never recovered. When she returned to her home she shut herself away in the women's quarters and from that moment she neither ate nor drank. Within four days she was dead.

Simut was heartbroken. The neighbourhood was stunned. Who could have believed that Takhenet's domineering character could so easily be shattered? One or two neighbours felt more than a twinge of guilt when they remembered how their quick tongues had added to the evidence which had brought the case to court. Several of Simut's friends could not bring themselves to look him in the eye, seeing his grief and knowing that their wives had contributed to it. The family drew in on itself. The planned marriage between Hari and Merytamen was postponed out of respect for Meryt's loss. She would have to look after her younger brothers and sisters now that their mother was gone.

Amenhotep went about his work in a subdued way, quick to anger at the smallest thing, intolerant of the slightest mistake by any of his staff. Though not foolish enough to voice their feelings in public, the brothers had always been passionate in their antipathy towards the royal family. This had been made more vehement by Prince Ramesses' high-handed actions, but the seeds of their discontent had been sown long before.

The Architect Ahmose, father of Amenhotep and Simut, had suffered in his day from royal favouritism. He had learned his trade on the building works at the Ipet Esut Temple under the King's father, the God Sethy, and had made rapid progress through the Royal Works Department until he became the architect in charge of designing and building the great Mansion Temple itself. He had given the best years of his life to the project and through it had hoped to make his reputation. But the King had appointed one Ameneminet, his childhood friend and army colleague, to be Chief Minister of Works in Waset with particular responsibility for the Mansion. Ameneminet had served throughout the King's campaigns as Commander of the Royal Chariot Division and had been the King's charioteer at the Battle of Kadesh, but he had little or no knowledge of administrative procedures and even less about architecture and building techniques. The civil appointment in Waset was no more than a reward for his military service. For the first years of his office he acknowledged his responsibility for the Mansion by no more than the occasional inspection tour, though he never bothered to acquire even a superficial understanding of working with stone. The real work was left in the capable hands of Ahmose and the organisational side of the royal building projects in Waset was dealt with by a professional administrative staff from their offices in the Mansion's Works Department.

Ameneminet's character had long been known in Waset, home of the Royal Chariotry, and as soon as his appointment to be Overseer of Works at the Mansion had been announced, the Architect had known that this bluff army officer would steal all his glory. The timing of the Charioteer's visits to his civil domain always seemed to coincide with some problem or difficulty which Ahmose would solve only to see the credit for his ingenuity go to Ameneminet. All the public acclaim for the work on the Mansion was for the Charioteer, while the honours, so the family believed, should rightfully have gone to Ahmose. Little slights and oversights, unthinking and uncaring words from Ameneminet and scant recognition for Ahmose's devoted service had built up a formidable edifice of resentment and blame. Ahmose included in his list of imagined wrongs the deaths of two daughters, one stillborn, and the resultant decline in his wife's health. All these events had contributed to an unreasoning hatred for everything that Ameneminet represented, even to the sacrilegious extent of blaming the King who had appointed the Charioteer to be Ahmose's superior. The Architect was a proud and conscientious man who had never given anything less than his best efforts in his work but a seething resentment festering in his heart had brought him to an early death. His family believed he had worked himself into the grave for the King. No wonder his sons were bitter. Ahmose, however, had been determined that his family should not suffer further and he had been able to make plans for their secure future once it became obvious that His Majesty had no concern for them.

Siamun and Haremheb cleared out Simut's storehouse since Simut himself could not bear even to enter the place until everything had been tidied and cleaned. When, at last, all evidence of Takhenet's folly had been removed, Amenhotep, Simut and the two young men gathered there to decide on their future. The fines levied by Prince Ramesses and the expenses incurred in Takhenet's funeral had used up a large part of Simut's available wealth. The storehouse was looking empty. Even the inner store had been depleted to provide, for her next life, those luxuries that Takhenet had always coveted in her mortal existence. Amenhotep arranged for a transfer of some basic commodities to tide the family over, but this would not be enough to restore the standard of living Simut had come to expect.

'You know what we have to do, Simy,' his elder brother said.

Reluctantly, Simut nodded. It was not that he had developed a conscience about the source of their wealth but somehow he had lost all interest in life since his wife's death. If it were not for the children he would quite easily have survived on a subsistence wage, foregoing the fine clothes and foods of his past, but Amenhotep would not let him slide into depression and self-pity. 'We'll go tonight,' he said.

'So soon?'

'It has to be now. We need to take advantage of a good moon. Besides, Prince Khaemwase is on his way to Waset and once he's in town we'll not get another chance until after the Jubilee.'

Simut shrugged his acceptance. The boys looked at each other in puzzlement until Siamun could no longer contain his curiosity. 'Where are you going, Father?'

Simut looked up sharply and said to his brother, 'Not yet, Ameny, don't tell them yet.'

'It can't wait much longer, Simy. We're neither of us getting any younger. We must tell them where we're going even if we don't tell them all the details yet.'

Simut grunted, still unhappy, but he said, grudgingly, 'I suppose you're right.'

Amenhotep took a deep breath and said, 'Boys, our father Ahmose has left us a legacy which is of greater value than anything you could imagine. He left us access to His Majesty's personal Treasury.'

Hari gasped but Siamun's expression remained calm. 'So that's it,' he said, 'I did wonder.'

'It's very simple,' Amenhotep went on, 'We can enter the Treasury without being seen. We could take whatever we wanted but we take only what we need.' He continued, describing how Ahmose, on his deathbed, had sworn his sons to keep the secret on pain of dire consequences when they met again in the next world. Obeying their dying father's instructions, Amenhotep and Simut had never taken so much as a single grain of gold from the Treasury, neither had they damaged any item within the King's personal storerooms. Such damage as the removal of precious inlay or metal fittings was too easily spotted, while the absence of a couple of jars from a collection of hundreds would hardly be noticed. The special rooms within their own storehouses had been prepared to hold the 'extras' as they called the purloined goods. For Amenhotep, Chief Designer in the Mansion's Building Department, apprenticed to his father almost from birth, such a project was scarcely difficult. Above all, they kept the existence of these cubbyholes from their closest relations. The occasional appearance of a jar of expensive ben oil or a bolt of linen could be explained as payment for a particular private commission or a bonus for a job completed ahead of time. There was, by unspoken agreement, no hoarding of unusable items.

'But we reckoned without Takhenet,' Amenhotep sighed.

To break the awkward silence, Hari asked, 'How much use has been made of this Secret?'

Amenhotep smiled, 'You see, Simy, I told you he was quick. We have been careful, Hari, believe me. We have taken only such things as we can easily account for or dispose of, nothing to raise the alarm or point the finger. We've not touched the jewellery, the furniture or the personal stuff. What we have taken has been replaced or its absence disguised so that a casual glance around the stores will reveal no glaring gaps.'

'What sort of things?' Siamun asked.

'Wines, oils, linen, leather goods, copper, bronze, it's all there for the taking, lad, and His Majesty rarely checks his possessions. The only time the seals are broken is when he has things to add to his hoard.'

'Or when there's a funeral,' Simut spoke for the first time. 'We had a nasty moment back in Year 25 when the King's Great Wife died. All her burial equipment was kept in the Treasury and the King himself came down to supervise the funeral arrangements.'

The boys nodded. The King had mourned deeply for his beautiful wife Nefertari. Her funeral had been the most lavish in Waset for years and her tomb was reckoned to be the most beautiful the Royal Workmen had ever made. 'Yes,' Amenhotep agreed, 'we couldn't go near the place for months. But even with all that activity going on, no one ever noticed there was anything missing. A little at a time is the secret, not too greedy, not too ambitious. What we've taken is hardly more than a fleabite, but then we've been careful not to draw attention to ourselves. We've lived a comfortable life, more comfortable, thanks to Ahmose, than we might have expected, and, I consider we've had no more than our due.'

Ahmose had seen his private enterprise as the provision of a pension for the support of his wife and children, a pension which he should have had anyway had it not been for the King's favouritism for his old crony. Ahmose had not lived to profit from his ingenuity but had passed on the knowledge of the Secret to his sons and had sworn them to keep faith with him and his ideals. They were bound not to reveal the Secret to another living soul until the time came when they thought it appropriate to pass on their father's gift to their own sons.

Their first raid on the Treasury had been an adventure, a trial run to prove what could be done. Simut and Amenhotep both felt their hearts beating faster at the memory of that escapade. They had wandered between the heaped valuables, fingering the fine cloth, breathing in the heady perfumes of spices and unguents, their eyes catching in every corner the glitter of gold. Once they knew what they had to deal with, they could make a plan of action and they had stuck rigidly to that plan for years. Each had taken an equal share of whatever had been 'liberated'. Their prizes were either taken across the river under cover of darkness or the goods could be secreted away in one of the sheds of the Works Department until an opportunity arose for them to be delivered, along with legitimate purchases and rations, to the brothers' homes in the Eastern Town. There they were placed in the family's stores, the most valuable and identifiable goods being hidden away in the secret compartments. Royal consumables had been enjoyed within the home allowing both men to developed discriminating palates for wine and the finer foods. Their wives and children were always immaculately dressed and their houses were well appointed without a hint of ostentation. Ahmose's legacy had provided extreme comfort if not luxury for his sons and they had cause to bless his foresight and his audacity.

Listening to their father's dispassionate admission of such bold thefts, the boys were amazed. They knew he was no lover of royalty but outwardly he had always appeared to be a loyal subject. Here he was almost gloating about how he and his brother had tricked the King out of a small fortune and he felt neither remorse nor guilt, only triumph. Simut looked less happy but now he had more reason than ever to resent the King's authority and he would support Amenhotep's actions. If anything, his attitude was even harder and less forgiving than his brother's.

Amenhotep finished his explanation with an apology, 'So you see boys, although our father never had the chance to make use of his Secret, he left his family well provided for. We are bound by the promise we made him and for now we can tell you no more. When the time comes, we'll show you the way in but for the while you must trust us.'

For a fleeting moment Siamun considered following Amenhotep and Simut when they went on their next raid, but he could not work out how to trail them across the river without being spotted. Besides, his father had asked for trust. In time all would be made clear.

The results of that particular visit to the Treasury were a small plank of resinous wood, some leather pouches of spices and dried herbs and two jars of ox fat. Every precaution was taken to avoid arousing suspicion. Each man could only deal with bulky or heavy items like the jars one at a time because they were awkward to carry and difficult to conceal. But a second trip a few nights later relieved the King of two more jars of fat, bundles of sweet rushes, a small sack of pure salt and a flask of scented oil. There was method in the choice of goods. The girls of both families were set to making festal perfume cones, rendering the fat, purifying it with an infusion of the rushes and scenting it with spices in oil or wood chips steeped in old wine. After boiling and skimming, the cooled mixture was shaped into conical cakes. With the Jubilee celebrations about to start, all manner of festival goods were appearing in the marketplace. None of the items from the Treasury was offered for barter in its original form. The delicately perfumed cones were soon exchanged for a variety of less spectacular goods, some of which were immediately traded again so that the family were seen to have 'earned' their quite considerable profit. By the time they were able to enjoy or make use of the fruits of their labour, so many transactions had taken place that the source of the original materials had been obscured and who was there to question the legitimacy of the trade? There was Sunero, of course.

*

The Spy felt he had to explain himself. 'I watched them. Hatiay watched them. They were so clever. I was looking for things I could identify, things that might appear on an inventory. I was expecting the odd bronze bowl or some fine linen. I never considered they might be processing their ill-gotten gains!'

The Count laughed, 'That was the skill of it. Not too much, not too greedy, not too obvious, like Amenhotep said. It had become a game.'

'A game worthy of Seth himself; clever, devious, cunning and, above all, annoying!' Sunero said with feeling.

Khaemwase came close to laughter himself at this exchange between his servants. 'Now, now, my children,' he said with a paternal smile, 'Let us not fall into recriminations. It is all so long ago. And now it is past midday. A meal awaits you. Return as soon as you can. This story is becoming interesting.'

Chapter Five

The afternoon session began with reminiscences of the Prince's arrival in Waset to proclaim his father's Jubilee. As the royal barge drew up to the temple quay at Ipet Esut, the trumpeters sounded the salute and the local garrison troops came to the alert. The gangplank was lowered and the Prince walked down it to receive the welcome of the Tjaty and the two mayors of the Eastern and Western Towns. Khaemwase was dressed as the Sem Priest of Ptah. His shaven head was bare of wig or headcloth, his heavily pleated gown was partly covered by a ceremonial cheetah-skin robe and on his feet he wore plain sandals woven from papyrus.

The Tjaty Paser, who had taken on the office of High Priest of Amen-Ra at Ipet Esut only three years before, was also dressed in his priestly garments. He was to conduct the Prince to the Temple where they would officiate together at the evening ritual. The following day would be declared a holiday. Outside the colonnaded hall which his father had added to the front of the great temple of Amen-Ra, the Prince would proclaim the start of the King's Jubilee celebrations and, within the courtyard itself, he and Paser would oversee the erection of the Djed Pillar, the symbol of royal stability. There would be hand-outs of sweet cakes and beer for all who cared to attend the ceremony and that evening there would be family parties throughout the city. The last person on Khaemwase's mind was Sunero.

It was not until three days into the Prince's visit to Waset that the Spy was able to gain audience with his master.

'So, Sunero, have you been enjoying your vacation here?'

It was clear from his casual tone that Khaemwase had not received the report of Takhenet's trial, so Sunero brought the Prince up to date, delivering his summation of events with typical economy of words. The Prince had no patience with rhetoric. At once Khaemwase's interest was rekindled. He trusted Sunero's judgement implicitly. If the Spy was convinced that a crime had been committed then it was worth a proper investigation.

'I think you should accompany me to the Treasury, Sunero. I have His Majesty's authority to choose gifts for the gods from his personal stores to celebrate the Jubilee. Let us see what may be seen.'

The King's personal treasure-house was in fact a suite of rooms within the Mansion Temple itself. Sunero, who was neither priest nor royalty, would not be allowed to enter the sacred areas of the Temple but, like the security guards, porters and maintenance staff he would have to enter by the side door in the southern wall. This admitted entry to the second court from a narrow lane which ran along the length of the temple between the holy precincts and the workshops and offices of the Works Department, including the stonemasons' yard where Siamun was employed. As it happened, Siamun was just leaving the yard as Sunero arrived and so the two men came face to face for the first time. The Spy recognised Amenhotep's son at once as he bore a strong resemblance to his father. Amenhotep's features had been burned into Sunero's memory at Takhenet's trial. The young mason, however, was completely ignorant of Sunero's very existence.

When they almost collided in the confines of the lane, Siamun looked the Spy up and down with a keen eye. He saw a man of medium build, medium height and unremarkable features, a veritable picture of ordinariness. It was the fact that Sunero presented such a nondescript figure that made Siamun notice him. As he later reported to his father, it was as if the man was trying very hard not to be noticed. 'He did nothing, said nothing. He was eminently forgettable. But he was *there* and I saw the doorkeeper admit him to the Temple. He wasn't a priest and he certainly wasn't a nobleman but he wasn't an ordinary man either. I can't say what it was about him but it made my blood run cold. We must find out who he is. Something tells me he's dangerous.'

*

Khaemwase smiled broadly, 'What a very accurate portrait; non-descript but dangerous. I like that Sunero. Who reported that conversation to you?'

'Baketamen, Your Highness.'

Khaemwase's smile faded. For a few moments there was an awkward silence. The Count shuffled his feet and Sunero shook his head to rid himself of painful memories. After allowing what he considered to be a suitable pause for Sunero to regain his composure, the Prince indicated that he was anxious to resume the story.

*

When Sunero found his master within the temple court, Khaemwase was talking with Harmose, the Chief Custodian of the Treasury.

'Ah, here is my man, Sunero,' he said as the Spy was admitted. 'This man has my *total* confidence and *complete* trust. Whatever he may ask or do he does in my name. Is that clear Harmose?'

The Custodian bowed. If Sunero was surprised to hear what sweeping powers he had just been granted, Harmose was furious. Since Khaemwase held the Royal Seal and was acting for his father, it had to be assumed that he spoke for the King. Harmose had no way of questioning or circumventing the Prince's orders. He would have to tolerate this nobody poking around and asking questions and, presumably, reporting back to the Prince. Harmose was not at all happy about this close scrutiny of his department. The Prince sensed the nascent animosity and tried to mollify the Custodian.

'Now, my dear Harmose, when was it that you last had cause to enter the Treasury?'

'It was last year, Highness, after the sad death of Prince Hun...' Harmose stopped mid-word. He had been about to say Hunchback, the apt if irreverent nickname which had been commonly used for Prince Nebweben, who had been born to a royal concubine before His Majesty had become King. The Prince had been cosseted and pampered all his life so that, in spite of his unfortunate deformity, he had survived to his thirtieth year before dying suddenly of a seizure. It had been planned that he would be buried in the Great Place, in the huge tomb prepared for those King's Sons who predeceased their father. A great granite sarcophagus was despatched to Waset and orders were received at the Treasury to withdraw certain funerary goods for Nebweben's burial. Harmose had overseen the choice of unguents, alabaster vessels and some furniture but in the event his efforts were wasted. The prince's mother, who had never carried another child to term, had begged the King to allow her to bury her son near her own residence in Mennefer, and most of the funerary goods were returned to the stores.

'So no one has been into the Treasury for over a year?' Khaemwase asked.

'That is so, Your Highness,' Harmose confirmed.

'Let us enter then, and see what gifts we may find which are fitting for the gods.'

Harmose led the way through a narrow doorway into the high, dark corridor which ran between the outer wall of the Temple and the southern side of the great columned hall. Bright daylight filtered through stone grilles set high in the walls but barely reached the floor. Harmose knew his way well enough in the dark but Khaemwase and Sunero were more cautious. It was just as well that the stone paving was perfectly smooth with no awkward joints or hollows to catch the unwary foot. At the end of the passage were the heavy, bronze-clad doors of the Treasury, guarded by two Temple doorkeepers who stood to attention facing each other across the doorway, their eyes studiously focused on nothing.

The entrance was lit by small torches set in stands to left and right, casting an orange-red light over the threshold and causing an unhealthy florid glow on the guards' faces. Harmose stepped aside and with a gesture requested that the Prince should inspect the seals. Khaemwase lifted the biggest of the heavy clay seals moulded around the strong cords which were bound over the bolts used to hold the doors shut. The clay was dried and shrunken, a network of small cracks had appeared on the rough under surface, but the impression of the Treasury seal bearing the King's name was clear and undamaged. The same was true of the two smaller seals. Clearly the bolts had not been drawn since Prince Nebweben's funeral. Khaemwase nodded his satisfaction.

The Custodian took a small knife from the pouch at his belt and neatly cut the cords and released the seals. At a word, the doorkeepers stepped forward and pulled back the huge wooden bolts which protested with a screech, setting everyone's teeth on edge. The massive door flaps were then pulled open, moving with only a hint of reluctance in their copper-lined sockets.

The air in the storerooms was warm and dusty, infused with every imaginable luxurious scent. There were no window grilles, only a few small ventilation holes at the junction between wall and ceiling. These were so narrow that the little light they admitted through the thickness of the walls was swallowed by the darkness of the interior and any breeze they might have provided was not strong enough to reach floor level. The Treasury was as secure as a tomb and just as dark and uninviting. The Prince would have entered at once but Harmose respectfully barred his way.

'We should wait, Highness, until the air has had a chance to circulate. In the farthest part of the storerooms it is quite possible to faint from the heat and airlessness.'

Sunero murmured his agreement. The Custodian knew his job. The Spy would be careful to cultivate Harmose's good opinion. The man's knowledge could be useful. At last, Harmose declared it to be safe and indicated that Sunero should take a torch. Walking slowly, with a kind of reverence, the three men entered the treasure-house.

Before they had gone beyond the pool of pale light spilling through the doorway, Sunero said, 'Stop!'

Harmose was about to reply indignantly to this peremptory order but when he saw that the Prince had obeyed his own servant he could not argue.

'What is it, Sunero?' Khaemwase asked.

'See the floor, Sir. See the footprints of those who came this way last.' The polished floor was obscured with a layer of sandy dust and clearly visible were the incoming and outgoing tracks of Harmose's porters, the footprints less thickly covered by the dust which had settled since the last visitors had made their exit.

'Where did your men go? What areas of the stores did they visit?' Sunero asked the Custodian, who reluctantly indicated the southern side of the main and largest room where furniture, coffins, chariots and other wooden goods were stacked.

'And then into the next room,' he pointed forward into the darkness, 'where most of the jars are kept.'

Sunero bent to study the floor. He pointed behind them, 'See, Sir, how our footprints differ from those made by the porters. If anyone had been this way since Harmose last sealed the doors, his tracks would be obvious. Maybe not as clear as ours but they'd be clearer than these. You can distinguish between the footprints left at different times by the way they overlap and by the amount of dust they've accumulated in the meantime.' He stood up and, holding the torch low and to one side he moved slowly towards the stacked furniture.

Harmose said sharply, 'I beg you, keep the torch away from the wood. Let me light the lamps.'

Sunero silently cursed himself for not thinking of this. Of course, the resinous woods in such a dry atmosphere would catch alight easily and burn away to ashes in no time. He said, 'I'm sorry, Harmose. I should have thought.'

Harmose grunted and, with a slight bow towards the Prince who stood still and thoughtful, he took Sunero to fetch lamps. They lit a couple of the largest lamps which stood in their own heavy wooden stands, and several smaller candle-lamps which could be carried. Then Harmose returned the torch to the stand outside the door before he was completely at ease. This activity had largely obliterated the year-old footprints around the stored furniture but the Spy was fairly certain that there had been no more recent tracks to be seen. Moving around the magnificent royal treasures he kept looking for signs of theft but found none. Tomb robbers, he knew, would strip the precious inlays of gold, silver, ivory and turquoise from such pieces, but he could find not the slightest gap in the elaborate patterns which bedazzled his gaze.

In one corner there were several chariots, dismantled, their wheels stacked together, their poles leaning against the wall. Every section was covered with gold, some embossed, some inlaid. Tomb robbers were known to burn such things and then recover the melted gold from the cold ashes of their fire, but a quick count reassured Sunero that all the parts of the chariots were there, unless a whole chariot had been removed, and that was impossible. Wasn't it?

He went back to the Prince who had remained standing in the central aisle of the storeroom discussing with Harmose the sorts of items he was looking for as Jubilee gifts. Their speech was hushed as if in respect for their surroundings but Sunero realised that the sound of their voices was muffled by the piles of wooden items filling the chamber.

As the Spy rejoined his master, Khaemwase said, 'Have you found anything?'

'No, Highness. May I presume to go before you into the farther rooms?'

'Of course. Whatever you think necessary. Lead on Sunero.'

The second room was only one third the size of the first but it was still big and was filled with jars of all sizes and shapes. They were in racks, they were on shelves, they were standing in rows on the floor or lying in neat stacks against the walls. Most were of pottery but some were of stone. Their necks were sealed with clay and almost all bore the imprint of the Royal Seal. There were oils, honey, fats and resins as well as every conceivable type of wine. On the shoulders of some of the wine jars were hieratic inscriptions giving details of the vineyard of origin and the vintage. Other jars were labelled with wooden tags hanging from cords tied around their handles.

The tracks of Harmose's workers were visible in the narrow alleyways between the stacks, but there was something else. Sunero's heart seemed to skip a beat. He had come to a pathway where there were no footprints. But there should have been footprints. He looked back the way he had come. Yes, the tracks came this way and there were the returning footprints of the porters who must have passed through on their way to and from the innermost reaches of the Treasury.

But the footprints simply stopped. He knelt down and carefully placed his candle-lamp on the floor. In its pale, orange light he examined the dusty paving stones. They were not as dusty as the floor over which he had just walked and the layer of dust had been swept into ridges which were unlike the natural settlement of dust which he had noticed elsewhere. Someone had been wiping out his tracks.

Sunero picked up his lamp and began a closer inspection of the jars. Those nearest to him were wide-necked vessels labelled as containing ox-fat. There were several rows of them, the dates on their shoulders showing that the oldest were farthest back in the ranks which Sunero, with his experience of estate management, thought was not the most sensible way to store perishable goods. Then he noticed another anomaly. Each row should have contained the same number of jars. Sunero could imagine Harmose's sense of order demanding this regimentation so that, even at a quick glance, any gap would have been immediately obvious. But the rows were not all equal. The jars had been subtly repositioned to conceal the fact that several had been removed. With his lamp held over the second row, the Spy could see, on the floor beneath the jars, the ring imprints which marked their original positions. When he looked again at the date markings, he found that some older jars had been brought forward to fill gaps. Reaching his lamp as far back towards the wall as possible, he could just make out the shadows which indicated the absence of jars. This was his first real proof that all was not well in the Treasury. Even on their brief acquaintance, he knew that Harmose would not tolerate such laxity.

Picking his way carefully so as not to destroy the visible evidence, he went to report to the Prince. Reluctant as Harmose was to accept Sunero's talent for observation, he had to admit that he would not have noticed the discrepancy in his stores. He was horrified and babbled his apologies, hardly knowing what to expect from the Prince by way of retribution.

Khaemwase attempted to put him at ease, 'Calm yourself, Harmose. You are not to blame. We think there is a very cunning plot afoot, perhaps a plot conceived years ago, before you became Custodian here. Now, Sunero, can we identify other losses?'

The Spy said, 'Whoever has been doing this has been very careful to cover their tracks, but it may be possible.'

They went through to the southernmost of the two remaining rooms where sacks, baskets and leather bags of all sorts of dry goods were stored. The signs were there too. Where Harmose expected to see his workmen's footprints the floor had been swept clear. Sunero pointed out where a bundle of spice sacks had been loosened so that one bag could be removed. The binding cord had been thrown back but had not been retied. Harmose regained some of his self-respect when he was able to show that the top plank from a pile of cassia wood had been removed.

'It was recently, too, Sir. See, the top surface is virtually free from dust while it is thick all around on everything else.'

The Custodian was at a loss to explain what was becoming increasingly clear to him. Over a long period of time, someone had been systematically and very cleverly robbing the Treasury. Without taking a complete inventory, which he had no right to demand, he would be unable to identify any future losses with certainty. Since no precise inventory existed, it was impossible to list what had already been taken. The realisation of what had been happening under his very nose made him shake with fear and, in no small measure, anger.

In the last of the storerooms, where the precious metals and sacred vessels and statues were kept, it was more difficult to say what might have been removed. There were no apparent gaps, though a basket supposed to contain a hundred copper ingots might well hold only ninety-five or even ninety before Harmose would be able to identify the shortage without physically counting the objects. Except for funerals and on certain religious occasions, there was no need to extract supplies from this part of the King's personal treasure-house. His Majesty's chief resources were held in Mennefer and Per-Ramesse. The last delivery to the Treasury at the Mansion had been when Prince Nebweben's funeral in the Great Place had been aborted and certain goods already sent to Waset from the North had been added to the King's stores rather than being made to suffer the return journey. Harmose knew, however, that his men had had no need to enter this room on that occasion. The last person to enter here would have been the King himself and that might have been as much as five years before when Queen Nefertari had died. The metal store was also free from all tracks. Even His Majesty's footprints had been wiped away. To Harmose this seemed like sacrilege.

'Well, I think we have seen enough don't you, Sunero?' Khaemwase asked.

'Yes, Highness. Our suspicions were correct.'

The Prince turned to Harmose, 'My agent will require your co-operation. Your meetings mut be discreet so you cannot use your own office, Harmose. Sunero has an office in the north administrative complex where you will meet him when required but you must not seek him out unless he asks for you because we cannot have the two of you seen together if we are to keep this investigation as secret as possible. Sunero will be reporting to me but he has my permission to inspect, interrogate, turn upside down if necessary, whatever and whomsoever he wishes. Do I make myself clear?'

'Perfectly, Your Highness,' Harmose murmured with a bow. His resentment at having this investigation imposed on him had been tempered by the Prince's insistence on discretion. If the Royal Heir considered such measures to be necessary the matter must be more serious than Harmose had imagined. If the Spy should uncover incontrovertible proof of a single theft from the Treasury, let alone thievery on a grand scale, Harmose knew who would carry the blame. He would have to sink his injured pride and deal with this Sunero as an equal.

'And now I must choose the gifts. Come with me Harmose. I will point out those things which you will have delivered to my barge. Sunero, you go about your investigations. I leave this matter entirely in your hands.'

The Spy also bowed. He was eager to tell Hatiay about his discoveries and felt he had seen enough of the storerooms for the time being, so he made his way back to the main doors. Then, just before the threshold he stopped. Clearly showing in the dust he could see his own footprints together with those of the Prince and the Custodian, and beneath them the partially dust-filled tracks of the last people to enter the Treasury on official business, tracks that had not been wiped clear. So the thieves had not come this way. But, if they had not walked along this aisle, through these doors, how had they gained entry to the Treasury? More to the point, how had they got their prizes out?

He turned and gazed thoughtfully into the gloom. Even the largest lamps cast but a pale light in the vast darkness. He could see little outside their tiny pools of brightness. The thieves would have needed lights. They would have brought something with them even as Harmose had brought the torch. Would they have had the audacity to use the King's own lamps? Why not? Not a glimmer of light would have been visible through the close-fitting doors to betray their presence to the guards outside. There were no windows through which a passer-by might have caught a glimpse of a flickering light and no lamp was bright enough for its light to be seen through those tiny ventilation openings. The thieves were audacious enough in targeting the Treasury for their crime. Burning a little royal castor oil would mean nothing to such men.

Sunero walked back through to the jar store and into the corner where he had first noticed the swept floor. It took only a short while to find what he was looking for, a lamp, a small, unremarkable pottery lamp, its wick almost burned away, its oil exhausted. It was nothing exceptional but it was in the wrong place. Just inside each doorway there was a shelf bearing a stock of such lamps. Harmose had collected theirs from the shelf to the left of the main door and presumably, when he and the Prince left the Treasury, their lamps would be returned to the same shelf. No servant under Harmose's keen eye would dare to leave a lamp anywhere other than the proper place and certainly no one would have dreamt of leaving a lamp burning unattended. This lamp had burned itself out and it had been left on the flat top of a wax-sealed honey jar. Sunero went down on his hands and knees to search the floor again.

He found nothing until, almost hidden where it had fallen or been kicked, between the jars, he came across a piece of charcoal no longer than the first joint of his thumb. He turned the fragment in his hand. It was only small and he could easily have missed it but he knew it was significant. It appeared to be a carbonised section of reed, the sort of reed that was bound into bundles to make torches. Since Harmose would never have allowed a burning torch this far into the Treasury, here was evidence of the source of the thieves' light.

Sunero sighed. He was closer to the truth, much closer than he had been when he first passed through those massive doors, but he was still confused. He was almost certain that the thieves had not used that impress-ive entrance. He did not even consider the possibility that Harmose had been bribed; that was a ludicrous idea. So the robbers had to have found another way in. But how? Where? Sunero was satisfied that he had proceeded as far as he could that day. After a good night's sleep he might be able to look at the evidence from a fresh point of view, assuming he could sleep at all.

*

'And did you sleep?' the Prince asked.

'I can't recall, Sir. Probably not, since I suffered many sleepless nights over this affair.'

'Go now, then, take some rest to replace that which you lost in my service. I am tired. I too will sleep. Come again tomorrow. Tomorrow.'

In the morning, however, Sunero and the Count were turned away from the Prince's door.

'His Highness has received a message from the King. No visitors today,' was all the doorkeeper would say. Sunero wondered what the King might be wanting of his son now. His Majesty was so healthy and so energetic that he had little patience with illness or infirmity. News of the apparent indisposition of his son and heir would have been most un-welcome. Perhaps the King was planning to visit Khaemwase, to remonstrate with him for what he considered to be nothing but weakness and indolence. It was just possible that such a tirade as the King was capable of delivering would jolt the Crown Prince out of his melancholy.

Sunero remembered hearing His Majesty shouting at one of his finance officers, a highborn personage and very quick to remind people of that fact. The King had told the man to 'Get your arse off that chair and do some real work for a change.' The man had been so startled by this display of the King's very human nature that he had resigned his post on the spot and retired to his country estate considering himself to be more a gentleman than the god he served.

His Majesty was now in his seventies and had celebrated his ninth Jubilee only the previous year, and yet he was as bold and brash as ever, and just as short-tempered. Apart from the obvious physical resemblance it was difficult to recognise the kinship between His Majesty and the Crown Prince. Khaemwase's mother, the elegant Isenofre, had passed on to her son her calm nature, her intellect and her patience. She had lived in the shadow of the Senior Queen, Nefertari, for many years. It was Nefertari who had borne the King's eldest son while Isenofre was the mother of the first princess and the second son, the soldier Prince Ramesses. While Nefertari took the position of prominence, accompanying her husband on all special occasions, being portrayed by his side on all his monuments, Isenofre kept her dignity and her hold over the King.

Nefertari had never liked Isenofre and had resented His Majesty's decision to have two Chief Wives, but as in all things the

King liked to be seen to do things better and more splendidly than any of his ancestors. Isenofre never pushed herself forwards, she had no need to prove herself and no wish to attract Nefertari's jealousy. When Queen Nefertari had died in Year 25 the King, seemingly inconsolable, had found solace in the arms of his surviving Queen. Isenofre was already in her forties by then, the respected and beloved mother of a talented brood of royal children. That she had, throughout those years in obscurity, kept the love of her husband, was proof of the Lady's strength of character which had been inherited by her son, Khaemwase.

But what the King had admired, even loved, in his wife, he could not respect in his son. The dead Prince Ramesses had been much more like his father, who had encouraged his son's military leanings and so caused somewhat of a rift between the boy and his mother. Almost in unconscious response to this subversion of her son, Isenofre had made every effort to encourage all those aspects of his younger brother's personality that were the very opposite of the King's ideals. Khaemwase had never been tempted towards an army career, despite having served the military apprenticeship which his father had made obligatory for all his sons, and having survived the near disaster of the Battle of Kadesh when he was still a child. Khaemwase had made his mark as an administrator, becoming the very antithesis of the brash, self-glorifying, larger-than-life character that was his father. The King could not deny his son's ability and had made full use of this talent, shamelessly exploiting Khaemwase's loyalty, but then he had never expected that this prince might be his successor.

Nefertari's eldest son had died in Year 20 and the position of Heir Apparent had passed to one of her younger boys, but by Year 25 he too was dead, soon to be followed by his mother. At last the way was clear for Isenofre's children and Ramesses became the Royal Heir. This suited both the King and the new Crown Prince and Khaemwase was left to follow his own inclinations. Prince Ramesses had seemed as indestructible as his father and the country settled down to the comfortable notion that the succession was secure and would be uncontested by either the priests or the nobles, and least of all by the royal family itself.

But the King had lived longer than anyone could have expected and Prince Ramesses himself had aged rapidly under his new responsibilities. When, in Year 50 of his father's reign, Prince Ramesses had died, the King would have liked to return the succession to Nefertari's children. But by that time they had all removed themselves from the mainstream of court life, some moving to estates in the provinces, others firmly settled in priestly or governmental careers. As far as the Court was concerned there was only one candidate for the position of Crown Prince and that was Khaemwase.

The Prince was not the easiest of people to work with but he was known to be fair and his knowledge and understanding of royal protocol and religious ritual were unsurpassed. He had stayed in the North, building his own villa in Mennefer and bringing up his family within a stone's throw of the ancient Royal Residence of Ineb Hedj. He may not be a soldier but in all other respects he was a perfect candidate for the kingship. In fact, his was the sole name to be mentioned by every adviser, every courtier and even every soldier when sounded out by the King in his search for an acceptable heir. The King had no choice but then neither had Khaemwase. He became Crown Prince and Heir Apparent and the country began to look to his children as Egypt's future.

Now that future seemed in doubt. The King would not permit such a self-indulgent show of weakness. Khaemwase would not be allowed to will himself to death. Sunero had hopes that the King's intervention might be what was needed but he also knew his master very well, perhaps better than His Majesty knew his own son. He recognised that stubbornness in the Prince's nature that could lead Khaemwase to die just to spite his father. And then what? Where would the succession go if Khaemwase finally gave up his spirit? Tradition demanded that the King be succeeded by a son. The title of Crown Prince would almost certainly pass to Khaemwase's next surviving brother who would have to be schooled in his new role just as all the other Heirs before him.

Despite the hordes of children fathered by the King on a crowd of lesser wives and concubines, there was no obvious choice of successor from among their ranks, and the truly Royal sons, the children of Isenofre and Nefertari, were all set in their ways. No one in the administration would relish the prospect of having to break in a new Crown Prince. Khaemwase had been the last realistic candidate for the Throne. His death would cause more upheaval than anyone would care to contemplate. No wonder the King was concerned.

The Count's voice jolted Sunero from his thoughts. 'Let's go and see the Apis.'

'Why not?' Sunero agreed. He had nothing better to do and a visit to his master's favourite place was always pleasant. Care of the Apis bull, reincarnation of the spirit of the Creator god Ptah, was one of Khaemwase's most important functions. He had been the Sem Priest of Ptah since his late teens and had taken this responsibility most seriously. A new Apis had been installed in the magnificent stables in the precinct of the Mansion of Ptah earlier in the year.

Sunero was recognised by the gatekeeper as Khaemwase's man and he and the Count were waved through. Leaning on the stout wooden fence surrounding the bull's exercise pen, the two men watched the creature with affection. Both had been involved in the search for the new bull. This young animal, not yet fully grown, was the fifth Apis of the King's long reign. The requirements for the bull's markings had been laid down most precisely in remote antiquity. The black and white animal had to have a patch shaped like a vulture with wings outspread on his back, a crescent moon on his brow and the mark of a scarab on his tongue. The hairs of his tail were supposed to be double but that was difficult to identify so any young bullock with a thick tail tassel would be examined. The Count felt a particular fondness for this animal since he had been the first to identify it. The calf had been born in his neighbour's cattle shed only three days after the demise of the old Apis. This in itself was a good sign. The god's spirit had not been left without a suitable body for too long.

'He's growing well,' the Count said with understandable pride. 'Here boy!' He held out a handful of sweet hay plucked from the stack in the yard. The bullock pricked up his ears at the familiar voice and trotted over to snuffle the titbit from his friend's hand. It was a comfortable life being the receptacle for the god's spirit. The Apis would have the best of everything Kemet had to offer a pampered bull. His servant priests existed to supply him with food, accommodation and, when he reached maturity, heifers. Cattle-owners would be queuing up to have their cows serviced by such a beast. The offerings to the temple by way of stud fees formed a quite considerable part of the god's income. And when the bull died, after a life extended by comfort and luxury, he would be buried in a magnificent basalt sarcophagus in the underground gallery designed to Prince Khaemwase's personal instructions. He would have the august company of the four Apis who had gone before him and would, in time, be joined by his successors.

As for human companionship, the Apis was thoroughly spoilt, having been reared by hand from his earliest days. The ritual of the Apis cult was performed by his own personal servants who were all ranking priests of Ptah. The animal was groomed and cleaned, and generally fussed over by his own stablemen who supervised his diet and kept his hide, horns and hooves immaculate. When the end came the Apis would have his Sem Priest for company in eternity, for Khamewase had built his own sepulchre at the end of the gallery tomb, disdaining the provision made for his burial in the huge tomb built for his numerous brothers in the Great Place at Waset.

But which would go to his rest first? At the moment it looked as if the Apis would outlive his High Priest. The bull could live to be twelve or even fourteen years old. Sunero could not see Khaemwase surviving the end of the year.

The Count was scratching the animal's nose and when he stopped the bull butted his hand for more.

'He knows who his friends are,' Sunero said.

'He's a sensible beast. The god's spirit is getting stronger in him by the day. He'll be a fine Apis, one the Prince can be proud of.'

'If he lives to see it. He hasn't shown much interest in this fellow so far, not like the others. When the last Apis died it was as if he saw it as a sign. He'll not get close to this one because he knows he won't be Sem Priest for much longer.'

'That's his opinion. I wonder what the King thinks about that.'

'I don't think it matters what the King thinks. The Prince has made up his mind to die.'

'You're convinced that we won't be able to change his mind?'

'We're only delaying the inevitable.'

'Well, we'd better practise our delaying tactics.'

Chapter Six

The friends were unsure as to what they should do the next day. Each waited in his own home, hoping rather than expecting to receive the Prince's summons. It did not come. Sunero tried to do some work but his heart was not in it. He delegated some estate business to his deputy and spent the morning reading through his personal record of the First Jubilee Year.

Before the Prince had left Waset he had given Sunero a written warrant confirming the broad powers and authority which he had already given verbally. Sunero had access to the Treasury whenever he wanted although, to counter any resentment, the Prince had stipulated that he should be accompanied by Harmose on every occasion. Having overcome his initial reluctance to accept Sunero's position, Harmose was prepared to help in any way he could. He was a worried man. He knew he should have seen the signs. It was his job to keep His Majesty's possessions safe and he had failed. It was a matter of professional pride that he should bring the culprit or culprits to justice.

The two men conducted a thorough examination of the Treasury. It took days. They drew plans and made lists of what they could see but Harmose was adamant that nothing should be moved so they could not check the contents of chests and could only estimate numbers of certain items. Harmose's reasoning was that what had been placed there by the King or his agents should not be moved except on similar authority and the Prince's warrant stopped short of specifying this authority for Sunero. The Spy was not over concerned by Harmose's very precise interpretation of the Prince's wishes for he saw sense in these restrictions. It was his observation of subtle changes in position that had confirmed the fact of the thefts. If they went through the whole Treasury re-packing and re-stacking then such clues would be lost amidst the general upheaval.

It was during this time that news reached Waset of the death of the Apis. It had been expected for some months. Now Sunero knew that his master's thoughts would be elsewhere. The problem in the Southern City would not be forgotten but it would be set aside. It was up to the Spy to carry on the investigation and to have reports ready whenever the Prince might require them. Apart from the examination of the Treasury itself, Sunero instigated a surveillance of Simut and his family. Hatiay coordinated this using as his spies clerks, servants and workmen who would not raise suspicion. They reported daily to him and he kept a detailed diary of the movements of every member of the family. His one concern was that he could not continue the surveillance at night. The streets and lanes of Waset, in both the Eastern and Western Towns, were so empty in the hours of darkness that any observer would quickly be observed. Amenhotep kept a bedroll in his office in the Mansion's Building Department which he often used when work delayed him past sunset. This was common practice among officials who were unwilling to risk a ferry crossing after dark. Hatiay was certain that the Designer relied on this customary behaviour to disguise the real reasons for some of his overnight absences from home. The proximity of Amenhotep's office to the Treasury suggested that it would provide an ideal temporary store for thieved goods. Observation of that area of the Western Town was all but impossible and Sunero had no authority to search those premises so, in the event of a theft being identified, there would be no way of confirming his suspicions.

Simut's office in the Ipet Esut temple complex was at least on the same side of the river as his house. Hatiay made discreet enquiries as to the practicality of using another house in the street as a base for his investigators but it was a close-knit community and he knew if he pressed too hard the news would quickly get back to Simut and Amenhotep. Like most well-to-do families in Waset, the brothers kept a small sailing boat for pleasure jaunts up and down the river and a pair of rowing skiffs which were used for fishing or fowling expeditions and for private trips between the Eastern and Western Towns. When necessary, Amenhotep and Simut could call upon the services of watermen who hired themselves out to private boat owners, though both were familiar enough with the local waters to be able to row a skiff across the river. Hatiay's surveillance team had watched the town moorings for a while but the watermen were a close-knit group who quickly identified the outsiders. The Scribe called off his men after one of them was thrown into the river for asking impertinent questions.

The Scribe had expressed to the Spy his frustration at not being able to check on the brothers' movements during the hours of darkness. 'If they are our thieves they must have a way of getting to the Mansion unnoticed and then getting their ill-gotten gains out again and back across the river. It makes sense to do this at night but there's precious little overnight boat traffic and what there is can be almost impossible to track. Once out in midstream a small boat is virtually invisible, even at full moon.'

Sunero understood Hatiay's problem. 'The trouble is we haven't found any pattern to the thefts. There's no way of predicting when a robbery is to take place.We can only wait until a theft is identified and that might be days after it actually happens. I agree that it's most likely to occur by night on one of the occasions when Amenhotep finds an excuse to sleep in his office. If Simut uses a boat to go and meet his brother I suppose he'd have to have a half moon at least, but that means they could pick any time within half a month. You've shown that observing them by night isn't practical so we'll just have to depend on Harmose's guards. Their complement has been doubled and the watch is to be changed twice every night to prevent the men falling asleep on the job. Meanwhile, we'll just have to continue watching the family by day. That's the best we can do.' But, in his heart, Sunero knew that it was probably not enough. The more Hatiay's reports proved what an ordinary, upright family he was observing, the more suspicious Sunero became. 'They must make a mistake some time. It's unnatural to be so, so...so very boring!'

Then it happened. Almost half a year after Khaemwase had returned to Memphis, as Sunero and Harmose were carrying out one of their regular inspections, they noticed the signs again. Harmose stopped dead, horror written on his face, and pointed wordlessly to the floor. It had been swept. Only a short time was required to discover some of what had been taken. Finger marks on the lid of a linen press showed that it had been opened. There was no way of telling what the original contents had been since the label on the chest read simply, 'fine linen cloth', without giving either the total length of material it had contained or the number of bolts. One or two or even three of the folded lengths of fabric might have been removed for all Sunero could see. Spools of linen thread were also missing. The lid of the basket containing them had been replaced slightly askew. Harmose was pretty sure that several soft kidskins also had been taken from the middle of a bundle which, to his now practised eye, looked thinner than it should have been.

'It's all such small stuff,' Sunero said, shaking his head in bewilderment, 'nothing that would be out of place in an ordinary household. It will disappear into the system and we'll never be able to trace it.'

Harmose was feeling sick. His stomach had knotted at the first sign that something was amiss, and now anger had made it worse. 'Who do they think they are to flout the King's authority so, to use this place as their own personal treasure-house? Who are they?' He was of the opinion that Sunero knew or suspected far more than he was telling. Harmose was unaware of Hatiay's part in the investigations and, in spite of his association with the Takhenet trial, Simut's name had never been mentioned in connection with the Treasury thefts.

The Custodian looked at the Spy, hoping for some sort of answer, but Sunero's face was impassive. All he said was, 'I'll get them, Harmose, I'll get them!'

Hatiay's informers were quizzed remorselessly but no one had seen anything. Sunero scrutinised Hatiay's diary each day hoping to catch the merest hint of a discrepancy or an inconsistency in the regular pattern of the lives so scrupulously documented. But he found nothing. Then, a month later, he saw it. He could so easily have missed it. The inocuous entry in the diary reported the visit of Amenhotep's wife Rai and Simut's daughter Merytamen to the weavers' workshop of the Mansion where they had ordered fine linen cloth for making festival gowns. The marriage of Meryt to Rai's son Haremheb had been set for the New Year. The clerk who had reported the incident had added a remark to the effect that the linen was probably intended for wedding garments. 'How much cloth does it take to make a festival gown?' Sunero asked Hatiay.

'I don't know,' the Scribe was puzzled.

'It says here they ordered three lengths. Does that mean three dresses or could one length do for more than one gown?'

'I've really no idea,' Hatiay said.

'Well, we need to find out. If I know anything at all about this family, they won't stint when it comes to new clothes for the wedding. If one woman has a new dress, they'll all have them. Let's see, there's Rai and her daughters, even though little Shery is hardly more than a child, that's four. Then there's the bride and her two sisters, that makes seven women to be dressed in style. And I'll bet that the men will have new kilts at the very least, if not over-gowns as well. You can't tell me that three lengths of linen will make that amount of clothing. They'll need to get more unless, of course, they already have it.'

At last Hatiay understood, 'The linen from the Treasury!'

'Exactly! Now, can we find out if they've acquired any fine linen cloth since the inventory was made for the trial?'

'I can't remember any mention of it in the reports,' Hatiay said, but he was already reaching for earlier volumes of the diary to check. By the end of the day the two men were convinced that the family had not traded for cloth of that particular quality in the last eight or nine months. Indeed the only mention of linen they could find at all was the exchange of some basket wares for the shroud used for Takhenet's burial. 'So, they must have acquired it elsewhere,' Sunero said with a satisfied grin.

Then Hatiay said, 'But we don't know what was in Amenhotep's storerooms. We never had an inventory of his belongings. They could just claim that the extra cloth came from his store. The three lengths of new cloth ordered from the weavers will go to Meryt and her sisters. The rest will come from stock. We can't prove anything.'

Sunero slammed his fist on the lid of the file box. 'Seth's breath, they've done it again!'

At the New Year Festival, Hari and Meryt were married. Sunero stood with the crowd of well-wishers as the marriage party processed from the Mayor's office where, as befitted their status, Hari and Merytamen had been formally recognised as a married couple. He listened with feigned indifference to the casual remarks about how happy the couple looked and how well Simut appeared to be in the circumstances. But he cringed at the repeated comments about the family's immaculate turn-out.

'Don't the little girls look lovely in their new dresses? Just what Takhenet would have wanted,' one old woman said.

'Yes,' her companion replied, 'Rai has really done them proud but then she always was a good needlewoman.'

Sunero studied the objects of their admiration. The women certainly were dressed beautifully in flowing pleated gowns with bright red sashes. The men, too, were smart in crisply starched kilts and belted overshirts. All the wedding guests were bedecked with garlands and every member of the family, even the youngest daughter, wore finely tooled kidskin sandals. He watched his evidence being paraded for all the world to see, grinding his teeth with annoyance. He could prove nothing. Now was not his time. He knew they would have to slip up sooner or later and when that happened he promised himself he would be waiting. For one instant his eyes met those of Siamun and the young man frowned. Not wanting to give Amenhotep's son the opportunity to remember where he had seen Sunero before, the Spy ducked behind a tall Nubian who was watching the wedding procession with eyes full of sentimental tears. Sunero was gone before Siamun's recognition could become anything more than a passing sense of unease.

*

When the summons came at last, Sunero and the Count were surprised. The interval had been a full ten days and in the meantime the Prince had been visited in turn by his sister Bintanath, who had taken on the role of Great Royal Wife after her mother's death, the Tjaty Prehotep, the latest occupant of the office held all those years ago by Lord Sethi, and by his eldest son, Ramesses. The last visitor, setting the whole household awry by his unannounced appearance, was the King himself. In the face of such a purposeful offensive, the Spy and his colleague could foresee two possible outcomes. Either Khaemwase would be dragged back into the world of the living or he would turn his back on life, determined to slip away to the next world beyond his father's reach. In either case, Sunero saw no further need for their story-telling. Waiting in the anteroom for permission to enter the Prince's private chamber, the Count voiced both their fears.

'If I had relatives like his I think these last few days would have driven me mad. I wonder how he looks?'

'I don't suppose he's any different,' Sunero said. 'He'll not be brow-beaten, even by the likes of them. He'll have listened politely, agreed with them, bowed to his father's authority, and now they're gone, he'll carry on exactly as before. He won't have promised anything.'

The Prince was lying on his couch in a pose almost identical to that which he had adopted on their first meeting. Sunero realised they had to start again in their attempts to catch his interest. The Count also sensed a need to startle the Prince out of his lethargy. He started to speak before Khaemwase could tell them to be seated.

'Simut died at the beginning of the next year, just after the wedding. He choked to death on a pigeon bone. It was so sudden that he'd had no chance to pass on the Secret to his sons. It left Amenhotep feeling very vulnerable. He was torn between his loyalty to his brother and his care for his own family. Should he give his sons the chance to benefit from his father's legacy, or should he abide by his promise to Simut and not tell anyone until the twins were old enough to understand

and be trusted with such a secret? Should he keep the Secret to himself and die with it, bury it forever?'

The Prince raised an eyebrow in query, 'And what was Amenhotep's decision?'

'He felt the family had not yet extracted full reparation for Ahmose's treatment by the King. Simut's death had shaken him, made him realise how easily it could happen to him. He had to pass on the Secret.'

'So, it has come at last,' the Prince sighed with satisfaction. Sunero made himself comfortable as the Count told his story.

*

Amenhotep spent the period of mourning for his brother locked in a personal battle with his conscience. Only four days after the funeral he called his sons into his study. His face was lined with sorrow and worry. His voice was quiet, almost muffled, so that the young men had to lean towards him to hear his words. 'It's time you boys should be allowed into the family Secret. I've spent long, wakeful nights wondering just what to tell you, how much to reveal. I've had to consider Ahmose's wishes and Simut's, and I have to think about you in particular, Hari, since you are the man of the house now with people depending on you. I owe it to Simut to see that his children are well cared for. I've decided I shall show you the entrance Ahmose made into the King's Treasury but that is only out of necessity, you understand. One man on his own can't manage the way in easily and would have real difficulty in getting out again by himself. I need someone to help me otherwise I would still be keeping my promise to Simut. As it is, I must insist that, while I live, you never go to the Treasury without me. It is a resource that must be husbanded like any other. Over-use will draw attention to it and casual use for the sake of adventure is what would most probably lead to our being discovered. I know I can trust you but I must ask you to swear that you will never tell another living soul about this except when and if you decide to pass on the secret to your sons.'

And Amenhotep made his sons swear by fearsome oaths that they would never speak of the secret entrance to any other person this side of eternity.

*

The Prince suddenly looked concerned and held up his hand to stop the Count. 'You must not go on,' he said, 'I do not wish to be the cause of breaking such an oath. For Amenhotep, I see it was the only way to keep faith with his father and his brother. The oaths were well considered and should not be set aside so casually. Keep your silence, my dear Count, I am not so inquisitive that I am prepared to put another's soul at risk.'

Sunero found he had been holding his breath in expectation of his friend's revelation. At last he expelled the air from his lungs in a long, low sigh. What now? Where could they go from here?

The Count looked thoughtful for a moment, then said, 'The oath did not cover demonstrating the Secret to anyone outside the family, only speaking about it. I could show Your Highness Ahmose's legacy. Come to Waset with us, Sir, and learn the whole truth.'

Sunero prepared for Khaemwase's wrath at such a presumptuous speech but instead there was a silence, as heavy and oppressive as the air in a tomb. Then, in a low voice like the whisper of a draught, the Prince said, 'I shall consider that possibility. Now leave me to think. Come again tomorrow, early!'

Once outside in the garden the Spy could contain himself no longer. He rounded on his friend, 'What possessed you to say something like that? The man is dying and you suggest a trip to Waset!'

'It's made him think. If he decides to go to Waset we'll have prolonged his life by months.'

'And he could just die on the river and then where would we be?'

'You worry too much Sunero. He's not as ill as you seem to think. In fact he's not ill at all, he's just sick at heart. I've offered him something that no one else in the world has and if it means going to Waset to get it that's what he'll do. He's sought knowledge all his life. He'll not pass up an opportunity like this, believe me.'

'I hope you're right,' Sunero said, but he sounded less than convinced. The Count slapped him on the back in a good humoured way. 'Don't lose any sleep over it. You'll see I'm right.'

But Sunero could not so much as doze. The events of that time kept flooding into his consciousness as soon as he tried to give himself over to sleep. It was not the excitement or the tension of those times that kept him awake. It was the unrelieved tedium of nothing happening and the soul-eating frustration of being unable to do his job.
He had sent a report to the Prince when Simut died. There had been a raid on the Treasury shortly after the funeral but, as always before,

neither he nor Harmose could find the entrance the thieves had used. They had both come to the inevitable conclusion that there must be an alternative entrance to the main doors. They had talked over the possibility of a tunnel but, as far as could be seen in the dim light that Harmose allowed, the huge flagstones of the Treasury floor were undisturbed and, they would have sworn, immovable. They had studied the external wall of the Treasury from the lane outside. They found no hidden door but that would have been too easy. The remaining walls were within the Mansion Temple to which neither Harmose nor Sunero had right of access. Only the priests and higher-ranking temple workers who had undergone the necessary purification rituals were allowed within the sacred precincts. Sunero was as confident as he could be that the entrance, if it existed, was not from the temple side of the Treasury. Indeed, even he was beginning to doubt that such an entrance was possible, and yet how were the thieves able to make free with the King's wealth if not by means of some secret door or passageway?

The goods taken on that occasion had been mere tokens. In fact, Sunero was almost willing to swear that nothing had been taken at all except that Harmose insisted that a jar of something and a bag of natron were missing. If the Custodian's suspicions were correct, given the lack of a proper inventory, other goods could have been taken without their absence being noticed.Sunero interpreted the visit as a proving run. Now he felt he knew for sure that Amenhotep was involved and he suspected the sons had been let in on the secret, but there was still no proof, only his intuitive belief.

The Prince had responded to the report in an unexpected way. He had summoned Sunero back to Mennefer. The Spy had been languishing in the obscurity of Waset for a year and a half and had nothing to show for his time there except his speculative reports. Khaemwase could no longer afford to waste a man of Sunero's talents. He had more important work for his agent to do and, although it irked him to leave a job unfinished, he was prepared to admit defeat, albeit temporary, in the matter of the Treasury losses. After all, the goods that had gone missing were almost unnoticeable within the totality of the King's wealth. It was more a matter of hurt pride than of real suffering, and His Majesty was, as yet, unaware that he was being robbed. His Majesty had far more important things on his mind. At last, as the final act of the Peace Treaty first drafted all those years ago after the Battle of Kadesh, a marriage contract was being negotiated between the King and the daughter of the Hittite ruler, Hattusilis.

Correspondence had been exchanged between the two courts for years. In the early period of negotiations, even Queen Nefertari had written to the Hittite Queen whose daughter was the object of Egypt's interest. While expressing her desire that the two royal houses should be united in joy at the proposed match, Nefertari must have been fairly confident that the foreign princess would never supplant her in the King's affections for the girl was hardly more than a babe in arms at the time. The Queen knew that the Hittite girl would be no immediate threat to her until she reached adulthood and that might never happen, for many children died young, even in royal families. The haggling, particularly over the dowry, had been going on for as long as anyone could remember. Many of the officials who had started the negotiations had died or retired without having an end to their labours in sight. Queen Nefertari herself was also dead before the foreign princess had reached marriageable age and Hattusilis had revived the more serious discussions. It seemed that the possibility of Kemet acquiring a Hittite Queen was coming closer and closer to reality.

On his return to Mennefer, Sunero was thrown back into the real world almost immediately. Khaemwase was very much involved in the King's marriage negotiations and, at the same time, was deeply concerned about his mother. Queen Isenofre was dying. Everybody knew that apart from the King, who refused to accept the inevitability of his wife's decline. Prince Khaemwase was of the opinion that the sudden revival of the marriage plans was his father's attempt to avoid dwelling on this painful reality.

Queen Isenofre was not insulted by the King's apparent eagerness to replace her, even before she was in her tomb. She knew her husband too well for that. Between the King's demands and his normal priestly and administrative duties, Khaemwase was unable to give as much time to his mother as he would like. He knew there was much to be done in setting her private estates in order so this was the task he set Sunero. In the next few months the Spy came to know and understand the Queen, and with that knowledge came a vast respect for the gracious lady who had lived on the edge of splendour for so many years.

When Isenofre died, Sunero begged the Prince to be allowed to accompany the Queen's body to Waset. Permission was readily granted but the Prince's party stayed only a short while in the Holy City. Sunero barely had time to consult with Hatiay and catch up on the latest news of Amenhotep's family. The Designer's eldest daughter Nefertari had married and had gone to live in her husband's home town of Suan.

'They gave her a grand send-off,' Hatiay said. 'Their sailing barge was laden with wedding gifts; furniture, household linen, kitchen utensils, just about everything for setting up a very comfortable home.'

'When was this?' Sunero asked. Hatiay looked back through his diaries to find the precise date. Within the hour the Spy was checking this date with Harmose. The Custodian had been keeping scrupulous records of what he could identify of the extractions from the Treasury, but even so he was convinced that more had been removed than he could account for by his simple observations.

'Of course, the Queen's funeral has upset all our arrangements. Things have had to be moved around a lot to get at her funerary goods. The coffins and such were stored a long way back so we've had to shift a huge amount of gear, but at least it'll be easier now to see if things go missing. There's less to worry about and gaps will be more obvious.'

'But what of this particular time?' Sunero persisted. 'It would be around four months ago, maybe a little longer, and there would probably have been more than one raid.'

Harmose checked his notes. 'Yes,' he said, 'there was a time, about half a year ago.' He searched for the relevant entry. 'Here,' he said triumphantly, 'linen, oils and a basket of copper tools one time, then, only ten days later, wines, spices and a sack of bronze ingots.'

'That's two heavy loads,' Sunero said, rubbing his chin in contemplation. 'I'd say our gang has increased in size or its members are suddenly stronger than they were.' In his mind he saw clearly a picture of the muscular Amenhotep with his two well-built sons. There was nothing he could do except to recommend Harmose to be vigilant, an unnecessary exhortation in the circumstances. Then he had to return to Mennefer with the Prince and at once he was plunged into another world, one in which the doings of an artisan's family in Waset had no place. At Khaemwase's bidding he was set to learning the Hittite language, both spoken and written, in preparation for a new role. He was to become a diplomat.

*

While Sunero lay awake remembering those in-between years, the Count was making love to his still beautiful wife. When at last they lay, her head resting on his chest, she asked, 'How did it go today with the Prince?' Her voice was deep and husky with a slight hint of a lisp. Although she spoke Egyptian faultlessly it was clearly not her mother tongue. The Count stroked her short-cut hair. 'I suggested he took a trip to Waset to see it all for himself.'

The woman sat up, the bed sheet slipping away to reveal small, neat breasts. 'You did what? The man is dying! How could you be so cruel?'

'You're as bad as Sunero,' he said, reaching out to fondle her nipple.

She pushed his hand away. 'For once Sunero is right. I don't think you realise how determined Khaemwase is. He has made up his mind to die.'

'So you think you know him that well still, after all this time?'

There was no hint of jealousy in the Count's voice and his wife read none into his words. 'A woman does not forget her first man. I was with Khaemwase long enough to understand the man within the Prince.'

'And then he threw you to the jackals, eh my sweet? Don't you feel at all aggrieved that he used you so?' There was a mocking tone to his voice.

'He gave me everything,' she said quietly and with great dignity. 'He gave me to you.'

He reached for her breast again and this time she did not object.

Chapter Seven

The two men were waiting at the Prince's gate at sunrise. Neither had slept much but each for a different reason. They had hardly exchanged more than a cursory 'Good morning,' when the gatekeeper summoned them in.

Khaemwase was breaking his fast, soaking pieces of leavened bread in his wine. There was an array of foods set out for him but he disdained them all. 'Help yourselves, my friends,' he said, waving his hands in an expansive gesture. The Count needed no second bidding. He scooped some curd cheese into a flat loaf and selected a fat gherkin from the pickle bowl. Sunero chose a date cake and some fresh figs which were not the sharp-tasting sycomore fruit but real figs from the Prince's own garden. The butler poured wine for both of them. It was warm and spiced. They ate in silence, the Spy aware that his master was studying them carefully from behind half-lowered eyelids. At last the Prince called for the debris of the meal to be removed and servants brought bowls of scented water and towels. When all was cleared away, Khaemwase leaned back in his cushioned chair and put his feet up on the high footstool.

'I have been considering your suggestion, Count, but I have not yet made my decision. I wish to know more, to know if this small matter is really worth my further attention, let alone my uprooting myself and travelling half the length of the country to satisfy a mild curiosity.' The Count grinned. He knew the Prince's curiosity was more than mild. 'So tell me,' Khaemwase continued, 'what happened after Amenhotep let his sons in on the family secret?'

*

The family continued to live comfortably but inconspicuously. Haremheb, now a fully-qualified accountant, took up a post at Ipet Esut as a Scribe of the Herds of Amen, the same position in which Simut had started his career. His first child was born shortly before his sister's wedding. The baby boy was named Simut. The betrothal of Amenhotep's daughter, Nefertari, to a ship's captain from Suan had necessitated several trips to the Treasury in order to augment her dowry and she was dispatched to her new home with a very generous load of bride goods and family gifts. Her brothers and her father had been exceedingly careful in their choice of goods, knowing that Nefertari's parents-in-law would examine every item. Nothing should be labelled with unusual marks or seals. Nothing should arouse suspicion or attract unwarranted attention. They were most successful. The general opinion, both in Waset and Suan, was that Nefertari was a very lucky girl, dearly loved by her family and with very generous relatives and friends.

In spite of the influx of materials taken from the Treasury, Nefertari's dowry had seriously depleted her father's stores and Amenhotep was just planning another trip to boost his resources when Queen Isenofre died. There was then so much activity in the Treasury, sorting and cxtracting Her Majesty's funerary goods, that Amenhotep and his sons could not risk the venture. For some months they dared not use the secret entrance and had lived blameless lives surviving off their standard rations.

*

'How I feel for you, my dear Count,' the Prince drawled, a curl of wry amusement hovering around his lips. 'It must have been so very hard for you all, having to work for your living for a change.'

'We had always worked, Your Highness,' the Count said with some asperity. 'No one could say we were afraid of hard work. We all took pride in our crafts, and we were good at our jobs. It's just that we didn't consider we were being properly paid for all our efforts.'

'And I suppose you thought you were still entitled to reap the rewards of Ahmose's little bit of insurance?'

'Exactly, Sir.'

'Shameless! Utterly shameless!' but the Prince's voice held the shadow of a laugh. 'Carry on with your story.'

*

To everyone's surprise it was the even-tempered, practical Rai who started to complain that life was not as comfortable as it had been. Things were brought to a head when Rai and Merytamen inspected the family stores with a view to planning a dowry for Meryt's sister Nofret.

'I was appalled,' Rai had told her husband later. 'I knew the stores had been run down somewhat since Simut died, after all Hari isn't bringing in the salary that Simy did, but even so it's a pitiful sight for Nofret when she's just seen Merytamen so well provided for. I offered Meryt some goods from our stores but I'm ashamed to see how Nefertari's marriage has left us so short. Could we not have managed things better?'

Amenhotep had little to say. He had hoped that strategic raids on the Treasury would have restocked his storeroom to a reasonable level but with the delay brought about by the Queen's death, the situation had deteriorated so far that even the inner store was less than half full. Although it was risky, especially since the doubling of the Treasury guard, and no one knew why that had been ordered, Amenhotep planned an ambitious series of visits and drew up a list of goods to be abstracted from the King's possessions. Within a matter of four months the family stores were substantially replenished. Nofret was married off in suitable style and even if her dowry could not compare with those of her sisters, no one could accuse Amenhotep of not caring for his brother's children.

*

'So that's why I was suddenly inundated with letters from Waset!' Sunero said. By that time his diplomatic duties had taken over his life and on the rare occasions when he found time to visit his old office, he had to be selective about the paperwork he chose to inspect. It would have been all too easy to become involved.

The reports from Harmose and Hatiay were filed, as he had ordered, without being read by his secretaries. He felt duty-bound to read them when he could, though they were often repetitious and usually extremely boring. Then, after a long period of inactivity, Harmose identified a rash of thefts and the list of missing goods was quite extraordinary. The Custodian's reports became more and more hysterical. Sunero drew one from the file box as an example.

The Custodian of the Treasury at the Mansion of His Majesty, Harmose, greets the Prince's agent, Sunero.

Have you not read my last reports? Have you not seen how vile thieves have again and again desecrated the private storerooms of His Majesty the King? Let it not be said that Harmose, the Custodian of the Treasury, had been lax in his duty. I have doubled the guard and I personally inspect the seals on the doors at all hours of the day and night. I have replaced the seals regularly using knots that only I can tie. Never have I found a sign that the doors have been forced. Nor have I found a man amongst my chosen guards who is corrupt or who would dare to enter His Majesty's Treasury unless I ordered him to do so. How then is this crime being committed and by whom? It is my belief that you, Sunero, know more than you have confided in me. I wish His Highness the Prince Khaemwase to know that I have done all that he asked but how can I do my duty when my hands are tied?

*

'You really treated the man very poorly, Sunero,' the Prince said. 'He was feeling bad enough about having you put in authority over him. Then you showed him how he had overlooked serious thefts and put his integrity in doubt. When he did his best to make up for all this, you ignored his letters. I think he had every right to feel aggrieved.'

'So do I, Sir. I would rather have stayed in Thebes with him and seen the business through but, if you remember, I was under Your Highness's orders to become a diplomat.'

'Ah yes, of course, the Hittite Marriage. How long ago all that seems. I suppose I did rather take you out of circulation, but you were by far the best man for the job. I needed my own man in the escort party sent to fetch the Hittite princess and I could trust no one else.'

'But the journey to Hattusas, the official handing-over ceremony in Amor, the exchange of gifts and then the return with that incredibly slow baggage train – I was gone for six months. And then, when I got back...'

'Yes, yes, Sunero. I monopolised your time once more. You became an indispensable member of Her Hittite Highness' household. It was you, as I remember, who taught her our language.'

The Spy bowed his head as if in modesty at the Prince's recognition of his good work, but for the first time in this story-telling he had been hurt by a pang of memory. He dared not speak, he could not trust his voice not to tremble. Tears threatened. Now he knew why he had been unable to sleep. His mind had dwelt on those frustrating nothing years simply to avoid the painful memory of what had followed. He had found the only woman he had really cared for and she had been so far above him that love was unthinkable. The Count, who knew a little of what Sunero must be suffering, stepped in. 'And don't forget that Takhepa arrived in the Princess's train.'

To the Count's amazement, a broad smile spread across Khaemwase's face. 'Ah, yes, Takhepa. What a delightful creature she was.'

'She still is, Sir,' the Count retorted, his voice coloured with the jealousy which he thought he had conquered long ago.

'Of course, but Takhepa at sixteen, my dear Count...' There followed a long silence during which Sunero was able to compose his face and clear his throat. He then took up the story again.

*

The Hittite princess had been sent to Egypt with an enormous dowry in the form of jewellery, clothing, precious metal wares, furniture, slaves, horses, chariots, cattle, goats; the list was impressive and the transport of such an awkward assortment of commodities through Canaan in the wintertime was a nightmare. Once arrived in Mennefer, the bride goods had been allocated to various storehouses in the royal residence cities and the livestock was largely donated to the gods, to be added to the herds kept by the temples. A large proportion of the cattle was earmarked for the god Amen-Ra and Haremheb was sent to Mennefer as one of a party of scribes from the god's cult temple in Waset. They were to make a count of the herd and to see to their distribution to the god's estates in the Northern Realm. When Hari returned to the Holy City he travelled on one of the barges taking the Hittite treasures which were to be placed in the safekeeping of the King's personal store in the Mansion. Another passenger on the boat was Sunero.

The Spy made himself known to Hari in the least of his capacities as the Prince's agent. A new High Priest had been appointed to the Temple of Ptah in Mennefer, the oldest national shrine in Egypt, and one of his first acts was to declare the Blessing of Ptah on the King. This was to be a countrywide year-long progress in which His Majesty would present himself for the god's blessing at each of the major shrines of the Great Artificer. Khaemwase, as Sem Priest of Ptah, had been delegated the job of organising this progress and one of Sunero's tasks was to see to the preparations for the ceremonies that were to be held in each of the Chapels of Ptah within the great temples of Waset. Of course, he also had instructions, while in the Holy City, to consult with Hatiay as to the management of the Prince's southern estates and his prime purpose, the one not vouchsafed to Hari, was to see to the installation in the Treasury of the Hittite goods.

Although Sunero had spent nearly two years in the highest diplomatic circles, he found little difficulty in returning to the guise of a middle-ranking scribe. As such he had much in common with Haremheb who was grateful for a congenial companion on the long, slow journey southwards. When Hari discovered that his new found friend had no firm plans as to accommodation he immediately offered Sunero the hospitality of his own home. Meryt was less than pleased to find that Hari had invited a house guest without forewarning her but she was like her mother in her wish to keep up appearances and when she found that Sunero was employed by Prince Khaemwase himself she could not have been more welcoming. In fact, she insisted that Sunero should be invited to the family banquet she had planned to celebrate Hari's return.

Sunero smiled ruefully at the memory of that meal.

The Spy knew by sight every member of the family, even though the younger children had grown considerably during his absence from Waset, and yet he had to feign ignorance and wait to be introduced to each in turn. When he was not told the names of the youngest children he had to remember not to refer to them by name in conversation. Amenhotep and Rai were pleasant company and Hari and Meryt were the most generous of hosts but Siamun was a different proposition altogether.

Sunero was not aware that he had done or said anything to arouse Siamun's mistrust but it was clear from the young man's curt replies to innocuous questions and his almost permanent frown of puzzlement that he knew, or suspected, something about the Spy's presence in the midst of his family. He had not addressed a single remark to Sunero all evening when it was time for Amenhotep and Rai to take their children home. Then, instead of following his parents, Siamun took the Spy to one side and said, 'Let's leave Hari and Meryt to get reacquainted. They've been apart a long time. Let me show you one of the most memorable sights of Waset.'

So it was that the Prince's Spy was introduced to Lady Menhet's House of Delights. Menhet was a tyrannical madame with hennaed hair and a taste for heavy jewellery. In the heart of the fashionable waterside district of the Eastern Town, Menhet kept the most exclusive whorehouse in Waset, if not in the whole of Kemet, and she imposed a strict code of conduct on both her girls and their clients. Most of the Young Ladies, as Menhet preferred them to be called, were of foreign origin, daughters of prisoners of war who had worked on the King's great building projects, or of mercenary soldiers drafted into the army of the Two Lands. There were Nubians, Libyans, Canaanites, Syrians, even one girl who claimed to be Babylonian though no one could either prove or disprove that claim. Since the very few native Egyptian girls in Menhet's care tended to conceal their nationality behind exotic dress and make-up, it was perfectly possible that the Babylonian was no more than a local girl hiding her shame behind a façade of outlandishness.

But it was admitted that, whatever their origins, the girls of Menhet's stable, besides being clean, were the most cultured, the most sophisticated and the most expensive in Waset. This meant that their clientele was generally of a high standard. No poor man could afford a night with one of Menhet's young ladies.

Once Sunero realised where Siamun was taking him, he felt a warm thrill of satisfaction which had nothing to do with the prospect of sexual gratification. If Siamun was accustomed to frequenting Menhet's house he must have more disposable wealth than either Sunero or Hatiay had suspected and the Spy was now certain that he knew the origin of that wealth. When Menhet greeted Siamun as a valued customer of long-standing and included his guest in the warmth of her welcome, Sunero knew he was right.

While the Spy's suspicions about the young stonemason were now confirmed, Siamun's suspicions about Sunero were, as yet, barely taking form. He could say nothing against the man since he hardly knew him but his annoying appearance at odd times and in odd places made Siamun uncomfortable. He was determined to find out more and his plan was simple. He would ply him first with drink and then with questions. In his experience, the pleasures of Menhet's house were the ideal means of loosening tongues. Siamun reckoned without Sunero's stone-hard will and determination. It was Siamun who first slumped to the floor, his eyes and his tongue befuddled by beer. As Siamun's chosen young lady helped him into the dark recess of her bed cubicle, Sunero idled away his time with a pretty young Amorite girl who was new enough at the game not to be too eager to take him to bed.

It was Menhet's custom to rouse all her overnight guests before dawn and to offer them breakfast prior to pushing them out of her door ahead of the sunrise. She was surprised to find that, to all appearances, Siamun's new friend had not left the communal lounge. His little Amorite companion was still asleep, her head resting on his shoulder. Menhet's business spirit began to assess how much she could properly charge Siamun for what amounted to one night's bed and breakfast accomm-odation with no extras. No one else had asked for the Amorite that night so she could not even demand payment on the basis that Sunero had deprived another customer of the girl's services. Menhet had no wish to drive away potential clients of good character by overcharging, especially on a first visit.

Once Siamun had woken up sufficiently to understand what she was saying she took him to a secluded recess and started to negotiate. From a leather pouch at his waist the young man brought out two necklaces made of multiple strands of cheap, glazed beads. These were of the sort commonly traded in the marketplace for all manner of goods and would not normally warrant a second look. Sunero knew Menhet would want more than that since she had a reputation for class to be maintained, but it seemed the necklaces were acceptable. Siamun dropped them back into the pouch which he untied from his belt and handed to the brothel-keeper. Then Sunero understood. The real payment had not been shown, it was in the bottom of the little leather bag. What could it be? What was small enough and yet valuable enough to pay for two of Menhet's Young Ladies? It had to be metal, ingots of copper or bronze, perhaps even nuggets of gold. Siamun was disposing of the proceeds of his family's theft through the agency of a citizen whose possession of such valuables would not be questioned. The fact that Menhet thanked Siamun without looking into the bag indicated to Sunero that this was a regular practice. How often had Amenhotep's son done the same? How much of the King's wealth had passed through Menhet's hands to become simply part of the national economy? Sunero had to shake his head in appreciation of Siamun's audacity and cunning.

A short while later they left Menhet's house together. Siamun had hoped to quiz his companion as to his plans for the day on the way to the nearest boat quay, which was outside the Southern Sanctuary Temple. Not wanting to be trapped with the stone-mason on the ferry crossing to the Western Town, even though he had intended to seek out Hatiay as soon as possible, Sunero said he had orders to report to some of the Prince's staff at the Ipet Esut Temple.

'So we must part,' Siamun said, 'but I'll see you again at Hari's place this evening.' It was not so much an invitation as a statement of fact. Sunero allowed himself to be organised. By becoming close to Siamun he could fill in some of the gaps in Hatiay's surveillance.

To avoid crossing Siamun's path again too soon, the Spy walked along the riverside path towards the northern ferry landing where he could catch the official transport to the quay at the end of the Mansion causeway. He made his way to Hatiay's office where the Scribe was very pleased to see him. They had two years or more of reports and correspondence to catch up on and Sunero saved his discovery of Menhet's possible involvement until the end of their discussion.

Hatiay looked astonished. 'We knew Siamun had a reputation as a ladies' man but you know how difficult it is to keep track of anyone by night without drawing attention to ourselves. It's hardly surprising that we never made the Menhet connection. Why, the crafty young...!'

'Exactly, and his appetite is his weakness, I'm sure of that. I don't know what it was he gave Menhet but it was small and it must have been valuable. Harmose's records might give us some ideas. Metal is my guess but if it was gold that would be something that Harmose is bound to have noticed. So far the thieves have been careful to steer well clear of the gold and jewellery but knowing Menhet's reputation, her demands might be just enough to tempt Siamun into becoming a bit too greedy. And when that happens I want to be ready for him.'

'We need someone on the inside,' Hatiay said thoughtfully. 'I'll see what I can do. There's a couple of Libyan girls who've been working on their own initiative, so to speak. I've turned a blind eye to their goings on so far but now might be the time to give them an opportunity to redeem themselves.'

'Good idea,' Sunero said, 'but tell them as little as possible.'

For the rest of the morning he was in conference with administrators and priests of the Chapel of Ptah at the Mansion Temple and then, after the noon meal he went to see Harmose. The Hittite goods had been lodged overnight in the wharfside stores, but now they were being delivered, there was so much activity around the Treasury that Sunero was able to slip in unobserved in the midst of the porters and pack donkeys. Harmose was in his element. His scribes checked each delivery against his inventory and allocated each item a position or space in his master plan of the Treasury. He had been forewarned and a great reorganisation had been necessary to make room for the new treasures. This was the opportunity he and Sunero had always wanted. Now Harmose knew exactly what was in the King's stores and where it was to be found. He wore a smug expression as he watched the Hittite dowry entering his domain and this became a broad smile of welcome when he recognised the Spy.

Sunero was very impressed by Harmose's scheme. 'Have you found any further discrepancies during this shake-up of the system?'

'Not much more than we suspected before,' Harmose admitted, 'but it will be much easier now to see just what goes missing next time.'

Harmose chuckled. 'I'd give a lot to see their faces when they find out how much things have changed since their last visit.'

Sunero noticed with amusement the Custodian's tacit acceptance that the thefts would go on. 'Could you show me around?' he asked politely, 'I'd like to get the lie of the land.'

'Of course,' Harmose readily agreed. In his tour of the Treasury, Sunero made many genuinely appreciative remarks about the hard work the Custodian had put in to rationalise and systematise the King's possessions. The first hall still contained the largest items, the furniture, chariots, coffins, planked wood, unworked ivory tusks and the larger, ornamental stone vessels. The second hall had been radically reorganised and the seals on all the jars had been checked. Cracked or leaking vessels had been disposed of and an exact inventory of what remained had been made so that Harmose could put his hand on any jar requested within a few moments of consulting the plan which he had personally recorded on a series of thin leather sheets. He pointed out the spaces left for the jars of precious Hittite oils which were soon to be delivered into his care.

The last two rooms had been tidied rather than reorganised. Sunero made particular notice of the removal of many layers of dust. Boxes and baskets were now labelled with wooden or ivory dockets listing their contents. Sunero lifted the lid of one basket to reveal a set of fine gauze linen curtains studded with gilded bronze sequins in the shape of daisies. The textile was not the sort of thing that could be traded on the open market but a few of those daisies, neatly clipped from the lower folds of the fabric, could be converted into superior costume jewellery, earrings perhaps or part of a bracelet. There was no record on the basket label of how many sequins were applied to the cloth. Harmose would never notice such a theft despite all his careful efforts. Sunero shuddered as he caught himself thinking like a thief.

Their inspection was interrupted at regular intervals by the arrival of yet more valuables to be stacked and stored away in the dark fastness of the King's Treasury. While they were surveying the richest prizes in the precious metal store, a gangling Nubian porter was ushered in by one of Harmose's subordinates. In one hand he carried a broad pedestalled bowl intricately chased in solid gold, supporting its massive weight in the crook of one sinewy arm. On his other shoulder he carried a jewel casket but, strong as he was, the Nubian was clumsy and as he set down the golden vessel where the guard indicated it should go, the box slipped from his grasp. It fell with an echoing crash, its contents spilling on to the newly swept stone floor. Harmose belaboured the porter with his tongue and his fists until the poor man was crouching with his hands over his head and weeping tears of pain and regret.

'Come, Harmose,' Sunero said, 'it was an accident. I think we'll find there's little damage done.' He persuaded the Custodian to inspect the fallen chest while the thankful Nubian beat a hasty retreat. One side of the wooden box had split but since it was reinforced at the corners with silver and bound with two metal bands, the box had kept its integrity and the hinges were undamaged. The jewellery was mainly of chunky stone beads, brightly coloured carnelian, turquoise and real lapis lazuli. The Hittites had chosen materials and colours which were known to appeal to Egyptian tastes though the workmanship was not as fine as that produced by Egypt's own craftsmen. There were bracelets, anklets and heavy necklaces, some with gold ball and cylinder beads interspersed amongst the coloured stones. The jewels had come to no harm as the several layers of kidskin in which they had been packed had cushioned their fall. Helping Harmose to pack the pieces back into the casket Sunero made a mental note of their shapes and patterns. It seemed to him that these gaudies had not been considered spectacular enough for the King or his new Hittite wife to wear in public, nor delicate enough to be worn in private. They were to be hidden away in suitably royal exile. Like the gilded daisies, they would be perfect prey for an enterprising thief. Each piece could be broken into its parts and restrung or reworked and combined with cheaper glazed beads to create new items which would bear little resemblance to the original Hittite monstrosities. The gold would attract attention in inappropriate hands but in certain quarters a few of the weighty beads could be passed, in the bottom of a small pouch for instance, with no questions asked. Sunero sighed as he began to see how the thieves worked their secret. It was ingenious, cunning and very lucrative.

The last jewel to be placed in the box was an unlovely necklace, a single strand of carnelian beads with a pendant plaque, also of carnelian, held in a gold wire surround. The plaque was carved with a sphinx shown in the Hittite style, winged and standing rather than lying down. It was a heavy piece which was unlikely to appeal to the stylish ladies of the royal household, though the plaque itself was of a particularly pure red and almost translucent stone. Separated from the beads the plaque had some merit as a work of craftsmanship but as a work of art the necklace had little to commend it.

Harmose studied the wooden chest and clicked his tongue with annoyance. Sunero tried to mollify him, 'The split will not be visible if you stack the box so.' He shifted the chest to the end of the shelf so that the cracked side was against the wall. 'It's lucky the Hittites thought to strengthen this box with iron.' He fingered the metal, cold and grey, and rougher to the touch than silver. Those two bands, each hardly broader than his thumb, were probably more valuable than all the contents of the casket put together. The Hittites had the secret of iron-working and controlled it restrictively. The flow of iron into Kemet was limited to ceremonial and small items, none of which could be converted to military use. It was the Hittites' iron weapons which gave them, in the minds of their adversaries, an advantage in the field of war. But that perceived advantage was of no importance to Kemet now, since the marriage was the culmination of the ultimate Peace Treaty. The Kings of Kemet and Hatti were brothers, allied forever against their common foes, just as Sunero and Harmose were united against their common enemy, the audacious thieves whose identity Sunero was now sure, beyond question, he knew.

'I see you have much to do, friend Harmose. I'll leave you to it. I don't think we will be troubled by our visitors for some time yet but I shall be staying in Waset for a while on the Prince's business so I shall speak with you again. I think the time has come to set a trap for our thieves.'

Harmose's face brightened at the prospect of action at last. 'Yes, I agree. All these changes have swept more than dust away from the Treasury. They have dispelled my feeling of impotence. We must catch these fiends. They have been allowed too much license for too long. I shall put my mind to the problem.'

Confident that Harmose would do just that, Sunero slipped away in the midst of a crowd of porters. Their way took them past the stonemasons' yard and the Spy could not resist a glance through the gateway but he could not see Siamun. There was a good deal of activity in a far corner of the yard where a crowd of workmen had gathered and there was much shouting and waving of arms but it was impossible to see exactly what was happening. Before he could extricate himself from the porters' company, Sunero found he had been swept past the yard entrance and to go back against the flow of the traffic in that confined lane was almost impossible. Even to try would have drawn unnecessary attention to himself, so he went with the crowd until he was back at the wharf at the end of the Mansion causeway. Hatiay had arranged for his usual rooms to be made available for the duration of his stay and he was still doubtful about imposing on Hari's hospitality, especially since Siamun was becoming suspicious of him. The unexpected expedition to Menhet's House of Delights had caused him to leave his few belongings at Hari's house so he would have to return there if only to reclaim his goods. The Spy knew that Hatiay would have been happy to provide a temple servant to go across the river and fetch his belongings but Sunero did not want his association with the Scribe to become known to the family. He would have to cross the river himself, make his apologies to Haremheb and Meryt and return. That would probably be for the best, he thought, in spite of the extra time it would take. He made his decision and set out along the riverside path towards the quay at the southern end of the Western Town where he could find a ferryman to take him across to the landing closest to Hari's home.

On his way he spotted a place where many small privately-owned craft were pulled up on to the muddy shore. He was not familiar with the everyday arrangements which the residents of Waset made for travelling between the two parts of their city. He had always used official transport and assumed that Hatiay and his colleagues did the same. Now he saw the rag-tag collection of reed skiffs and flat-bottomed lighters, rowing boats and scruffy barges, he began to understand how Amenhotep and his family could slip across the river unnoticed. He sought out the waterman who seemed to be in charge of the motley fleet. After some discussion he discovered that, for a small charge, any competent oarsman could borrow a craft to take himself across the river. The journey completed, the rower would leave the boat at the equivalent mooring on the eastern bank. For a higher fee, the traveller could engage the services of one of the boatmen who spent their days plying such vessels across the river or up and down stream to small waterside settlements. They were in great demand, the waterman said, especially when villagers had the odd sheep or goat, or baskets of vegetables, or a crate of pottery to be taken to market.

The old man laughed off Sunero's enquiry as to what the arrangements were for travelling after dark. 'If you're daft enough to try it you do it at your own risk. None of my men will row you.'

'But,' Sunero persisted, 'what's to stop someone helping himself to a boat when you're not here?'

'Nothing,' the man said.

'So is there any way of knowing if a boat's been used overnight?'

'Well, occasionally a boat turns up on the wrong side of the river, or goes missing altogether. There's always some young hothead who'll take a dare or try to impress his girlfriend, and others with criminal intent, hiding their doings under cover of darkness. We can't be held responsible for that sort of thing, and the owners know the risks.'

Having been given much food for thought, Sunero walked on to the official quay to take his boat. On the way across the river his thoughts came together in a most satisfactory fashion. He and Hatiay had assumed the thieves would be using their own boats to make their night-time crossings of the river. They had given no consideration to the possibility that Amenhotep and Simut might have used one of those communal craft. It was not surprising that the investigators should have been unable to spot any suspicious boating activity. They had been looking in the wrong place.

When he reached Haremheb's house he found it empty and silent and no amount of hammering on the door could rouse a response, yet surely there should have been at least one servant at home preparing the evening meal. Sunero made his way around the back alleys and found the rear gate. Sure enough, in the little kitchen courtyard an old woman was hunkered over the hearth, tending a large pot of bean and mutton stew. The appetising smell made Sunero conscious of his hunger. As he entered the yard the cook looked up and recognised him as the guest her master had brought home the previous evening. Before he could ask where everyone was, she wailed, 'Oh Sir, oh Sir! Have you news? Do you know anything of what has happened?'

A coldness gripped his insides. The prickling of hairs rising on the back of his neck gave him a sense of dread. He crouched down by the old woman and said, 'I know nothing except that I am hungry. Where is everyone?' The cook was evidently hard of hearing. She tipped her head and leaned towards him, 'Eh?'

'Hungry,' he rubbed his stomach.

'Oh, for sure, Sir.' She reached for a flat loaf from the stack set ready for the family's meal. Splitting it expertly she spooned in a good helping of the savoury stew and handed it to Sunero. In between bites he prompted her to tell him what she knew, which was little enough. Only a short while before he had arrived, a messenger had come from the Lady Rai to say that the family was required at once, something about an accident. It took several repetitions of the same question to elicit the information that the accident had involved the Designer Amenhotep. Hari had sent Meryt with the younger children to his father's house while he went with his mother. They were probably crossing the river at that very moment.

Sunero was hardly a friend of the family. Indeed he had only been known to most of them for less than a day. He would not intrude on the family's anxiety and yet he had to know what had occurred. The person to see was Hatiay. A messenger had already reached the Lady Rai so, by now, the Scribe would have had reports from his spies if anything unusual had happened in Amenhotep's family. After cadging a jar of beer and a handful of dried fruit from the old woman, he made his excuses and went to fetch his possessions.

He was not in too much of a hurry to notice that his bundle had been searched. To the unpractised eye it looked the same as it had done the previous evening when he had left it leaning in the corner by the front door. But the cords had been retied with a common knot which was unlike that which Sunero used. He was glad that he had maintained the habit of keeping personal documents with him at all times. The Prince's warrant and other precious papers were folded flat and kept within his broad belt. Siamun must have come back to the house as soon as they had parted company after leaving Menhet's place. He would have found nothing to belie what Sunero had told Hari about himself. The Spy wondered whether he would have escaped so lightly if Siamun had not fallen victim to the pleasures of Menhet's whorehouse. If their roles had been reversed, if Siamun had kept his wits while Sunero slept in a drunken stupour, the incriminating papers would doubtless have been found and read. It would be best not to tempt fate again. The Spy could not stay in Haremheb's house. He swung his pack on to his shoulder and went out by the back gate.

It was past sunset by the time Sunero reached Hatiay's office, but the place was still buzzing with activity. The Scribe saw his friend enter and called out, 'I wondered how long it would be before you turned up. Have you heard anything?'

'Only a vague mention of an accident. Tell me more.'

Hatiay took a deep breath before revealing his stunning news, 'Amenhotep is dead.'

*

The Prince held up his hand for Sunero to pause in his narrative. 'That seems to be a suitable point at which to stop for now. Go, stretch your legs, have something to eat and drink. I shall retire until the evening. Return to me just before sunset.'

Sunero bowed himself out with a sense of relief. It had been a painful morning for him as far as memories were concerned and now his lack of sleep and the emotional strain of his story-telling had combined to make him very tired. The Count, too, was subdued. The two parted with barely a word and each made his way home. On entering his lonely house, Sunero had just time to warn his servant to wake him before the sun was on the horizon, then he fell on his bed and was instantly asleep. Mercifully, his sleep was dreamless.

Chapter Eight

Showered and wearing clean clothes the Spy felt better when he and the Count presented themselves in the Prince's hall that evening. Khaemwase was lounging on a couch and drinking wine which he offered to his guests. As they sipped the honeyed vintage, the Prince said, 'I have been thinking about your proposition, Count. Perhaps you are right. I should see for myself. No story-teller, however skilled, is a substitute for one's own senses. Make preparations for a journey to Waset by the fastest possible means. I have not that much time to spare.'

Sunero blinked as, in an instant, the Prince's plans were laid open to him. Khaemwase meant to die in the Holy City. His burial place had been prepared within the catacombs of the Apis Temple so, if he died in the south, there would have to be a magnificent funerary voyage to bring him back to Mennefer. That would be something to make the King realise how much his son was appreciated by the people and something that Kemet would not forget quickly. Khaemwase was preparing for his own immortality, under his own terms.

The Count smiled, 'I shall see to everything, Lord.'

The Prince nodded, 'Now continue with the story. How came Amenhotep to die?'

The Count's smile faded and his head dropped but he started to speak in a low voice which commanded attention.

*

Amenhotep had been inspecting the huge stela which was to be erected in the Great Artificer's Chapel at the Mansion to commemorate the Blessing of Ptah. The stonemasons, Siamun included, had made a fine job of shaping and smoothing the stone. Now it was the Designer's job to set out the decoration and the arrangement of the text so that it could be carved and finished. No one could say what happened. Quite suddenly, the stone which had been wedged upright so that its final appearance could be better imagined, groaned and fell. Siamun inspected it later and the only thing he could suggest was that the wedges on one side had been made of a crumbly limestone which had given way under the weight of the stela. Or perhaps the wedging had not been properly done. However it happened, Amenhotep was crushed. The stone caught him on the shoulder and the side of his head as it fell, pivoting on one lower corner. A workman who rushed in to help, his arms raised in a futile attempt to take the stone's great weight, was also killed. Amenhotep lived long enough to call for his son. His last words were, 'Keep faith, Siamun, abide by your oath.' No one but the young mason understood what the Designer was saying.

The family was in such a turmoil of sorrow and anger that no one noticed Sunero's departure. After a suitable period during which Amenhotep's body was handed over to the embalmers and his funeral arrangements were set in motion, Sunero presented himself at the house to pay his respects to the family and to express his sympathy. Rai was flattered that the Prince's Man, as she called him, should remember them after such a brief introduction. Siamun looked on with growing concern as his mother talked and talked to the man he mistrusted, hearing her outpouring of the most intimate family details. For her it was a relief, a way of coping with her grief. To Siamun it seemed that Rai was including Sunero in the family where he had no right to be, and yet he still had no reason, apart from his instinctive suspicion, to believe that Sunero was anything other than he purported to be.

Forty days after the accident, Amenhotep was buried in the family vault beside his parents and Simut and Takhenet. By that time the family had a little bit of news to cheer them up. Meryt was expecting again. Hari promised that if the child was a boy he would be called Amenhotep.

Sunero had spent much time in the Designer's house at the express invitation of the Lady Rai who found him 'a most congenial person and so understanding.' She would hear nothing bad said about him and since Siamun still could not define his suspicion, he could not forbid the Spy entry to the house of which he was now the master. He also had to watch as his sister, Baketamen, became more and more besotted with the Prince's Man and, encouraged by her mother, began to talk about marriage.

Baketamen had been close to her father and had been devastated by his death, though she had tried to be strong and supportive for her mother. She had come to look upon Sunero as someone detached to whom she could unburden herself of all her pent up sorrows. To him she confided her feelings of helplessness and anxiety for the family's future, feelings that she could not admit to her mother or brothers. As Sunero had proved to be a sympathetic listener Baketi found more and more opportunities to talk with him and the attachment, on her side at least, had formed almost imperceptibly but conclusively.

It was with great surprise that Sunero found himself looking forward to his visits to the family home. His feelings for Baketi were confusing. He cared for her in a brotherly way, he enjoyed her company and she had the knack of making him smile in spite of himself, but was this enough to be called love? Baketamen clearly thought it was. Sunero, who had never expected to love anyone again, went through a lengthy period of doubt, examining his motives, trying to decide whether his loyalty to his master stretched to marrying into the very family he had set out to destroy. Baketi was a sweet girl and for her sake and that of her mother, both of whom, Sunero was convinced, knew nothing of their menfolk's nefarious activities, it would be a blessing to take her away from the scene of possible trouble. But lingering in the shadows of his conscience was the thought that the dowry provided for Baketi could prove to be very revealing. This made him hold off from proposing marriage and led to a stormy scene between himself and Siamun, who accused him of playing a cruel game with his sister's affections. To delay matters further Sunero then used the excuse that he would have to seek the Prince's permission before he could marry, which was true. But Sunero only needed the Prince's approval for this particular marriage, not marriage in general.

Since Khaemwase was soon due to arrive in Waset with his father for the Blessing of Ptah, it seemed sensible to wait and speak to the Prince in person rather than risk the crossing of letters and even more delay. The news that Sunero was important enough to require such permission elevated him still further in the opinion of Rai and her daughter but, at the same time, Siamun's suspicions became deeper and more worrying. He was no spy and he had no one he could trust to ask questions on his behalf except Hari. When telling his brother of his fears he was aware that he could put no substance to them. He could not point to a single word or deed of Sunero's that justified his suspicions, but Hari knew his brother well and if Siamun was concerned then he was prepared to accept that there was something to worry about.

Hari was better placed as a scribe in the Temple to find out about the Prince's Man. He discovered little except that Sunero was well respected and that the open-ended commission he held from the Prince empowered him to do almost anything Khaemwase might ask of him. The one thing that Haremheb found out that made him believe that Siamun might have some grounds for his suspicions was that Sunero was a particular friend of the Scribe, Hatiay. Having been dismissed from his job after Takhenet's trial, Hatiay had re-emerged as another trusted and influential employee of the Prince. He had offices on both sides of the River which, Haremheb's contacts suspected, he shared with Sunero. This news made Siamun swear.

'I knew it! That man is dangerous. I knew it the moment I saw him hanging about outside the Treasury. Hatiay got too close but I thought we were past worrying about him. Now he reappears and in partnership with Sunero. That's a powerful combination, Hari. We must beware.'

'Are you going to allow him to marry Baketi?' Hari asked.

'If he asks I can hardly refuse since it will mean he's already told the Prince. The last thing we need is to offend Khaemwase by suggesting his man isn't good enough for our sister. And besides, Mother would create an unholy stink and Baketi would probably cry herself to death.'

'So, what do we do? The stores are low after Father's funeral. We haven't his income to rely on any more and Mother will expect to provide a good show for Baketi. Can we risk a visit to the Treasury so soon?'

'We'll have to, and it'll have to be more than one visit, but it will be difficult with Sunero hanging around.'

'Yes, I think you're right. Do you know what Khaemwase's people call him?'

'Surprise me!'

'They call him the Prince's Spy.'

*

Khaemwase chuckled. 'Yes, my faithful Spy, the best among my servants. I sent you into an almost impossible situation, didn't I? I don't remember asking you to marry into the family, but I do remember that I thought it was a very good idea. I remember Baketamen too, a dear girl, and I think she genuinely loved you. You did well to take her away from the influence of her relatives.' Turning a meaningful look on the Count he said, 'He saved her much grief, you know. She could not have expected more.'

The Count bowed his head and said nothing. Khaemwase glanced up at the window grille showing black against the darkening western sky. 'I will let you go now,' he said. 'You may still have time to set those plans of yours in motion, Count. I shall look forward to hearing about them tomorrow.'

That amounted to their dismissal. As they left the villa, neither man felt much like talking. Too many memories had been stirred up during the day. Memories of love and death, sorrow and fear. They parted at the road which led down to the dockyards. Sunero nodded as the Count turned towards the River and then went on his own way to his empty home.

*

The next morning, Sunero waited for a while outside the Prince's gate but the usually prompt Count failed to appear. The Spy guessed that his friend was engaged in making the travel arrangements with which he had been charged the previous evening. When he decided he had waited long enough, he sought entry and was directed immediately to the Prince's presence chamber.

'No Count this morning?' Khaemwase asked, arching his brows in a questioning manner.

'No, Sir. I think he's preparing the boat for the trip to Waset.'

'Of course. We shall excuse him then. In fact, I am glad to have you alone for a while. There are some things that I think must be said between us which do not concern the Count.'

Sunero was rather surprised but his expression, long-schooled in the Prince's service, was impassive. Khaemwase continued, 'I have been reminded in recent days just how much I have relied on you over the years. I have been a hard master – no, don't deny it. I have always expected the very best efforts from my servants and I have little patience with inefficiency. I realise I have asked of you many things which were quite beyond the normal duties of an agent, no matter how devoted a servant he might be. You have never questioned my demands and you have always given me your total commitment and, more than that, your loyalty. I really had no right to make such demands on your conscience as well as your time and yet I accepted the fruits of your labours casually, as if I had every right to them. I am sure I never thanked you, so I am thanking you now, especially for what you did for my mother. I could not let anyone know how much it distressed me to see her suffer. I could not deal with her business myself as a son should have done. It hurt too much. That is why I asked you. I know she wanted me to convey her, and my, gratitude to you but somehow I found I could not do it. The way in which she spoke of you, the warmth in her voice – well, I suppose I was jealous. I should have told you about this long ago, but I kept in my heart her good opinion of you as if by not telling you I could keep it for myself.'

Sunero was feeling most uncomfortable as his master freed his soul of the burden he had carried for so long. He could not let Khaemwase go on. 'Please, Sir, there is no need...'

'But there is,' the Prince insisted, raising a hand against Sunero's objection. 'You do not know it all. The Queen made provision for you in her will, as you know, but you have never been fully informed as to the nature of that provision. You are a wealthy man, Sunero, but the knowledge of the full extent of your wealth has been kept from you. As executor of the Queen's estate, I was fully aware of what she intended for you but I have deliberately withheld it. I knew that the legacy my mother left would have given you complete independence and I did not want to lose you. Instead, I bound you to me ever more tightly, emphasising the master-servant relationship, pretending that what few gifts I allowed you from her bequest were really from me. I know now that I was trying to deny the feelings of friendship and, yes, even love, which my mother had expressed for you. I recognise my jealousy now. She looked upon you as a son and I have not been able to own it before. I have done you a great wrong, Sunero, and I beg your forgiveness.'

'Sir...I...there is no...I cannot let you say these things. What I did for Her Majesty I did not only out of duty but out of respect for a very gracious lady, and – yes, Sir – out of love. I cannot tell you how much it gladdens my heart to know how she thought of me. What she left me in her will is of no importance. The very fact that she remembered me at all was an honour beyond anything I could have dreamt.'

Khaemwase smiled, 'You are too good, Sunero. I see now what my mother saw in you and what I only ever half understood before. And I didn't allow you time to grieve. I packed you off to Hatti. I ordered you out of my sight while still keeping a tight hold on your reins. I needed to feel in control. You were the best man for the job, there can be no doubt in anyone's mind about that, but I have to admit that my reasons for sending you went far beyond the expedient and the diplomatic. In truth, I exiled you. I am not sure I will ever know the full significance of those months in the wilderness and the effect the whole business had on you. I know you were a different man when you returned to my service and I regretted what I had done more than I have been able to express. Then I flung you back into the entanglement in

Waset. I thought you needed taking out of yourself, you needed to return to the real world. Did I do right?'

The Spy had been given so much to think about that he could not answer. Silence hung about the two men like an early morning mist over the River, slowly lifting as the sun warms the air. It was the Prince who broke the silence with a quiet, gentle voice, 'I know, Sunreo. I know what I did to you. Some of it showed yesterday, although I realise I can never know everything. I do have eyes and ears and I do have feelings. But you have ever been a free man, Sunero, no matter how closely I bound you in my affairs. I would not like to think that I coerced anyone, least of all you. Tell me, did I really force you into a marriage you did not want?'

The Spy took a deep breath before answering in an equally quiet and controlled voice, 'No, Sir. Of my own will I chose to marry Baketi. I won't say that my reasons for marrying her were purely personal, nor can I put my hand on my heart and say that I truly loved her, not then. She was a sweet girl and I came to love her, in time, though I believe she loved me better than I deserved. I felt somehow responsible for her. When I really got to know the family, I was torn between my duty to you, My Lord, and my respect and affection for the innocents who were involved unwittingly. The Lady Rai and her daughters knew nothing about Ahmose's Secret. Their menfolk had guarded it too well. I found I had an opportunity to save Baketamen at least from the shame and scandal I was planning to unleash on the family. I had to do it.'

'I am glad it was that way, Sunero,' the Prince said with a half-smile, 'I would not like to think that you gave up a chance of happiness for my sake. I worried that Baketi was an expedient and that by marrying her you might have denied your real feelings, perhaps for someone else.'

Sunero gulped. The Prince was too close to the truth. Above all else, the Lady's name and reputation must be protected. He had no way of telling from Khaemwase's expression how much, if anything, the Prince really knew or merely suspected. He had to change the subject. 'Baketamen and I were happy in our way. I could ask for nothing more, and the wedding proved to be the beginning of the solution to our puzzle.'

'Yes, of course. You were right. The dowry had to be found. Tell me what happened.'

*

Sunero had received an urgent message from Harmose. There had been a theft, the first for several months and the Spy was asked to investigate. Harmose had arranged to meet him at the side door, as usual, although Sunero felt uneasy about this approach to the Treasury as it was too close to the masons' yard for comfort. So far, his association with Harmose was a well-kept secret and he had no wish, at that precise moment, to run into the brother of his future wife. Harmose's agitation was enough to put his personal worries to the back of his mind. 'I can't understand it,' the Custodian wailed, 'It's just uncanny. I'd swear that, apart from myself, no one, nothing, not even a mouse has entered that place since we finished installing the Hittite goods. How do they do it?'

'Show me,' Sunero said with crisp authority. He was in no mood to deal with Harmose's hysteria. The floor had been overlaid with a thin layer of dust since last Sunero had visited the Treasury. The only visible footprints along the central aisle of the first hall were those of the Custodian. Harmose placed his foot in one of the marks to demonstrate this to the Spy. 'There are no other marks until we get to the next chamber, then they're everywhere. I couldn't believe my eyes when I came in to inspect the place yesterday. It can only have been hours since they left.'

Sunero studied the tracks carefully and had to agree with Harmose. Although the culprits had passed and re-passed the main gangways several times, there was no newly settled dust in their footprints. In the further reaches of the Treasury, there were fewer tracks and he was able to identify two distinct sets of prints. One was larger than the other and the owner of the large feet was also flat-footed. Sunero stooped over a particularly clear set of prints and held his lamp close to the floor. He let out a low whistle of satisfaction. 'Look, Harmose!' Across the heel of one print was a line. 'That's proof!'

'Proof of what? I don't understand.' Harmose was too agitated to think clearly.

'It's a scar, Harmose. Our thief has a scar across the heel of his left foot. See, the line is repeated here...and here. This is not an accidental accumulation of dust. This is an identifying feature. They've made a big mistake.'

'But unless we catch someone, how does this help? We can't go looking at every left foot in Waset,' Harmose said with exasperation.

'We don't have to,' Sunero said, and he was thinking, 'We only have to look at two.'

Harmose was still not convinced, 'I don't see how it helps us now.'

'They've been careless. On past occasions they've swept their tracks clear. They've never left us this sort of clue before. If they can make such a simple mistake, then we stand a real chance of forcing them into a final, fatal error. Have you decided what was taken?'

Harmose looked brighter, 'Yes. At least, I've made a quick check of the obvious. It's pretty ordinary stuff but it amounts to quite a haul. There's linen missing, not woven cloth but balls of coloured thread, almost a sackful, and a bundle of kidskins, the whole bale this time. Some small bags of herbs or spices have gone too, though I haven't found out exactly what they took. I think they've had a set of bronze awls and chisels with good wooden handles, and some packets of needles of all sizes. I'm sure they must have taken more because that lot would not overburden them. They've taken far more on previous occasions.'

Sunero had to agree. It did seem a small haul and not too heavy for two strong, young men. Surely they had taken more. 'What about the jewellery and the precious metals?'

'Their tracks are all over the metal store, but I haven't had a chance to check properly. To tell the truth, I was scared of what I might find so I waited for you.'

'Well, we'd better go and look,' the Spy said and the two men strode with purpose into the innermost chamber of the Treasury. Harmose was right, the thieves had left their tracks everywhere, but there was no obvious sign that they had disturbed the King's most precious goods. The thin film of dust on the golden vessels showed that none had been touched, but on baskets and reed boxes it was more difficult to discern fingerprints. Sunero tried to remember the place as he had last seen it and realised that it was an impossible task. 'Can you see anything that's different, out of place, anything at all?' he asked Harmose.

The Custodian replied in a tone of desperation, 'No, nothing, and yet why did they trample all around here if they didn't take anything?'

Sunero studied the goods heaped on the floor, the baskets and boxes jostling each other for space on the shelves. How could he tell?

Then he remembered the Hittite jewels. Those, at least, he could be sure of recognising. He moved to the corner where the iron-bound casket had been placed and, as he identified it, his heart seemed to rise suddenly to his mouth. 'Harmose, look!'

The Custodian hurried over. 'Have you found something?'

'I'm not sure. Look at that chest. Do you remember when the porter brought it in? He dropped it and we had to repack it.'

'Yes, I remember. But it's still here. It doesn't look to me as if it's been moved. Do you want to look inside?'

'Look again! Remember! The fall caused one of the side planks to split. See, there.' Sunero pointed to the obvious crack in the wood.

'Yes, but what does that...' Harmose's voice trailed away to silence. Then he almost whispered, 'We hid the split by turning that side to the wall. Someone has turned the box around.'

'Exactly. Can we look inside?'

'Your commission allows you to do anything.'

They took the box down from the shelf. Sunero told himself not to be too hopeful but he was sure the box was lighter than it should have been. He lifted the lid. It had been skilfully done. At a glance the box was still full and, just showing beneath the first layer of wrappings, the hideous beads were instantly recognisable. Sunero sniffed. As he pulled back the kidskin, a strong smell of herbs arose from the casket. He lifted out a plain necklace of gold and lapis lazuli, too valuable to be taken by thieves who would not be able to dispose of it without arousing suspicion, and from below the next layer of leather, he pulled out two linen pouches. 'Here are some of your missing herbs,' he said to Harmose who sat back on his heels in amazement.

'The crafty bastards!' he said. 'So they took some jewellery and filled up the space with stuff taken from elsewhere in the Treasury.'

'I told you they weren't stupid. We would never have found this if we hadn't known about the box. How many other boxes were treated the same way? How many sacks of herbs are missing?'

'I can't be sure.'

'Then we'll have to check.'

It took them the rest of the day. By the time they emerged from the Treasury, their eyes bleary from working in the flickering lamplight, they had identified four further instances of herb pouches being substituted for jewellery, as well as being fairly certain that many more chests had been opened or moved. Harmose's careful labelling of the containers made it clear that the thieves had chosen for their loot ordinary pieces of faience or simple stone beads.

As they walked out, Harmose said, 'We'll never be able to identify those things. Even if one of those armlets was waved under my nose I'd not be able to swear it came from here. And if they restring them, make up different pieces, we'll have no chance of recovering a single bead.'

'That's how clever they are,' Sunero said. Then he paused as something else occurred to him. 'What about the gold? Many of those necklaces and things had some gold in them.'

'Not enough to matter,' Harmose said with a dismissive wave of his hand.

But Sunero was suddenly alert again. 'No, think about it, Harmose. One or two gold beads here, ten or twelve there. Consider how many pieces they've taken. Add it all up!'

The Custodian stopped in his tracks. 'By the gods, you're right. Melted down it would make two, maybe three palm-sized ingots.'

'Yes,' Sunero said thoughtfully. 'They wouldn't try to exchange gold beads openly. They'd either have to hide them away and not risk trying to trade them at all, or they'd melt them down and convert them into something more manageable. Now I can't imagine our thieves passing up an opportunity to make a profit. Where could they get rid of that much gold without getting caught?'

'They'd have to find a goldsmith who didn't ask too many questions, and that's not hard to do. Tomb robbers seem to have no problem disposing of their loot. They wouldn't get the full market value but it would still be worth it. There's a sort of unspoken code of conduct within the criminal classes. The goldsmith wouldn't talk and the thieves would keep their contact secret so they could use him again.'

Sunero agreed. Harmose had the right idea but the Spy suspected there was one link in the chain that the Custodian had not considered. He knew his thieves well enough by now to know that they would never act so directly. They would not put everything at risk by approaching a dishonest goldsmith in person. They would work through an unsuspecting third party. He recalled immediately the picture of Siamun handing the pouch to Menhet. Gold in the hands of a notorious madame; no one would question where she had obtained it, or from whom. But what did Siamun get out of the deal? Unlimited credit?

Sunero laughed aloud at the thought and Harmose gave him a hard stare. They were outside the Temple precinct by now but the Custodian still considered his companion's behaviour to be unseemly.

'I'm sorry, my friend,' Sunero said, throwing his arm about Harmose's shoulders, 'but I'm happy. They have made their first real mistakes and more will follow. We have them, at last, we have them!'

The Prince slapped his hands on his thighs. 'Were you really that confident, Sunero?'

'Yes Sir. I knew, then, that it was only a matter of time. There was no need for me to trap them or entice them. They would have incriminated themselves, in time.'

'But then, like the loyal servant you are, you reported everything to me and I put pressure on you to bring the whole business to an end.'

'Yes Sir,' Sunero said with a sigh.

'I must explain,' the Prince began.

'No Sir, you should not explain anything. You were, and are my Lord.'

'For once, Sunero, I disagree with you. You have served me faithfully for many years. I have asked of you things that I had no moral right to ask. You have earned my undying gratitude ten times over. You have even saved my life and, more than that, my reputation, and yet I have never expressed the true depth of the debt of gratitude I owe you. You have given unselfishly of your time, your effort and your pain on my behalf and I have repaid you miserably. I owe it to you to explain. Your loyalty does you great credit but now the end is very near and I feel I must justify myself before my friends as, shortly, I shall be required to justify myself before Osiris.' He raised a hand to halt Sunero's immediate protest, 'No, Sunero, no more pretence. Forget the difference in our rank. We shall all be as each other before Osiris. I shall just go to meet him before you. I call you friend and that is what I consider you to be. You are even more than that. As I learned from my mother, you are more a brother than any of my true brothers. Friends, brothers, should not have secrets from each other.

'When I went with my father, the King, to Waset that time, we found the Lord Tjia was failing in health. His decline, indeed, was so rapid that he had become convinced that he would never see the King again this side of death. His Majesty always had a soft spot for his sister's husband and was upset to see him in such a state. Tjia was of his generation and had married his favourite sister in a time before the family had become royal. Despite the fact that the Princess had died many years before, my father still thought of Lord Tjia as an older brother. The King had already reigned for more than thirty-five years. It was a sharp reminder of his own mortality.

'Tjia was becoming senile, rambling in his thoughts, muddling past and present, the living and the long dead. On one occasion when I accomp-anied His Majesty to Lord Tjia's quarters, the old man was ranting about the Takhenet trial. He was swinging between cursing Hatiay for wasting his time and questioning his own wisdom in dismissing the case so quickly. Clearly Hatiay's case had made a greater impression on him than any of us knew. It had been playing on his mind for five years. When my father, the King, heard his brother raving, he asked me if I knew anything about the case in question. You must understand, Sunero, His Majesty asked me direct and specific questions. I have never been able to lie to my father. I did not tell him everything but he is sharp-witted. He knew I was hiding the whole truth. He at once made the connection with the Treasury. He said to me, "You have until the New Year to catch these criminals. No one steals from the Lord of the Two Lands." You see, Sunero, I was under direct royal command. I, too, am but a servant of His Majesty. That is why I had to go behind your back.'

Stunned by such a confidence, the Spy could say nothing. There was a long and uncomfortable silence. Then the Prince's Steward announced the arrival of the Count.

Chapter Nine

The Count's arrival dispelled the sense of intimacy that had surrounded the Prince and his servant for a short while. Sunero found himself brushing imagined specks of dust from his kilt, anything to avoid having to look the Prince directly in the eye. Khaemwase shook his head as if to rid himself of his solemn mood and when the Count entered, he said, 'My dear Count, so you are here at last. I suppose your lateness has been to some purpose.'

'Yes, My Lord,' the Count said brightly, 'We may set sail for Waset whenever Your Highness wishes.'

'You have been busy, but we also have not been idle. Sunero has continued the story up to the time when I intervened to speed up the investigation.'

'Oh, yes. That was the first raid after the Hittite goods were delivered, the raid that provided for Baketamen's dowry.'

Sunero frowned. It was unnecessary of the Count to rub salt into the wound. The Prince, however, wanted to know more. 'Just how were those goods converted?' he asked, settling back in his chair to listen.

The Count sat down casually on a floor cushion and began to describe the events leading up to Sunero's wedding.

*

Distributed among many craft workshops and placed in the hands of women skilled with the needle, the kidskins and coloured threads were quickly turned into a wide variety of desirable and exchangeable goods, from workmen's loincloths, purses and pouches, to embroidered belts and finely woven tapestry work. Rai and Baketamen themselves worked some of the threads into multi-coloured decorative bands for the family's wedding clothes. Ever practical and economical, Rai renovated and restyled the clothes made for Nefertari's wedding. No one could accuse her of a lack of care for her fatherless children or criticise her management of the family resources which, as everyone in the neighbourhood knew, must have taken a downward turn since Amenhotep's death. The jewellery, as both Harmose and Sunero had predicted, was broken up and shared out between several jewellers and bead-workers, a small quantity to each. Some of the resulting pieces were given to Baketi on her wedding day. Most of the remainder was traded in the market place over a period of many months. As for the gold, Sunero was right. Menhet had long before come to an agreement with Siamun, She received the little metal ingots and took them to her usual contact, who asked no questions and expected no explanations. Menhet kept a careful tally of her exchanges and, in accordance with an unspoken but binding business arrangement, she took a portion of the returns as her commission. Because Menhet was a recognised professional person in whose hands it was not exceptional to find copper or silver, or even gold, she obtained proper professional exchange rates with the goldsmith, far better rates than the brothers could have obtained on their own behalf. In this way, Menhet had become the family banker.

Amenhotep had not known that his sons had started extracting gold from the Treasury. It had been one of Ahmose's prime directives that no gold was to be taken, but the temptation for the two young men, when faced with such riches, was too great. They had wanted to make up for lost time and when their father had died they had become even more determined to make the King pay for their grief. Sunero and Harmose had miscalculated. The gold beads and chains taken in that one raid had made six good-sized ingots, a fortune for any ordinary man but hardly a drop in the lake of the King's wealth. The family's fortunes were to be restored gradually so that their mother and sisters, Meryt and the children should never suspect anything.

The wedding was celebrated in slightly subdued style but no one could say that the family had not done their best for Baketamen. Until his return to Mennefer, when his new wife would obviously accompany him, Sunero moved into Haremheb's house. It had been agreed that Baketi should help Meryt with the household until the baby was born. Meryt was not having an easy time with her second pregnancy. She needed a lot of rest and having her sister at hand to take charge of little Simut relieved her of one burden. In fact, Meryt became so ill that it was decided that her twin brothers, still only ten years old, should be found lodging with relatives elsewhere. One of Takhenet's brothers, who had long ago disowned her for marrying into a lower class, at last acknowledged his family ties and offered the boys a home. As Rai said at the time, his agreement to the arrangement had more to do with the fact that his wife had produced only daughters so, by adopting the boys, he could provide for his as well as their futures. The twins moved into the comfort of a small country estate and were immediately so spoiled that they would never want to return to the City.

There remained only the youngest sister, Tiye, and at eleven years of age she was almost an adult. Meryt could not bear to lose her and Tiye had no wish to leave. Tiye and Baketi between them took over most of the everyday household chores allowing Meryt to become a lady of leisure, a role in which she was not altogether comfortable. Sunero and Hari were quite glad to be out of the house for most of the day, leaving their women-folk to argue over who was allowed to do what. Despite their care and the removal of family pressures from Merytamen, Baketi and Tiye were unable to prevent the tragedy. Meryt had gone up to the roof to check on some herbs she was drying, but the climb was too much for her. At the top of the stairs she felt suddenly very faint and cried out for Tiye to come and help. Her sister arrived, but too late. Meryt had fallen. She was found crumpled at the foot of the stairs. Her neck was broken. The baby died with her.

*

'That death could not be laid at the King's door,' the Prince said. 'You cannot say that a raid on the Treasury was apt revenge for the loss of Merytamen.'

'No, Sir, maybe not,' the Count said, 'but at the time it seemed like a way of relieving our anguish without hurting anyone else.'

'And in the end, you hurt only yourselves.' The Prince clapped his hands together to signal the end of the story-telling session. 'I have decided. We shall go to Waset with you, but I have one request – no, in fact, I insist on this one thing. Takhepa must go with us. We shall leave at dawn the day after tomorrow.'

The Prince's tone brooked no argument. The Spy and the Count knew they had been dismissed. They bowed their way out of the room. In the garden, the Count cursed under his breath.

'What are you moaning about?' Sunero asked him. 'You wanted this trip, or didn't you expect him to accept the offer?'

'Why does he want Takhepa?'

'He doesn't want her. He gave her up years ago, but, as you said yourself, she's part of all this. He'll want to hear her story from her own lips. You realise we'll have to stretch out the tale to entertain him all the way to Waset. We'll need Takhepa. She'll be a great help, believe me.'

'You're probably right, but I don't think she'll like it.'

'You have no choice, neither has she. Now, I have things to set in order at the office before I can go gallivanting off on a river voyage. I suggest you break the news to Takhepa as quickly as possible then give some serious thought to who else you are going to invite along with us.'

'Who else do we need?'

'I knew you wouldn't have thought this through properly. The Prince can't go unattended, he'll need at least a body servant and, I would suggest, a doctor. Then there's the cooking. You can't expect the Crown Prince of Kemet to live on sailor's rations.' Sunero had to smile at the bewildered look on his friend's face. 'I suppose I could sort out the Household personnel if you deal with the crew and supplies. It's just as well His Highness doesn't want to leave immediately. Enlist Takhepa's help, that will soften the blow.'

The Count looked unconvinced but with time now limited, he had to take control of the situation and make the most of it. The two men discussed the trip to Waset as they walked through the town towards the Mennefer dockyards. By the time Sunero left his friend at the gateway to the Royal Quay they had thrashed out the skeleton of a plan and each had a firm idea of his part in the organization. Sunero walked back to the administrative quarter composing letters and memoranda in his head as he went.

Before dawn on the day of sailing, Sunero made his way to the Royal Quay where the Prince's boat was moored. They had decided to commandeer Khaemwase's personal barge for the voyage. While not the fastest vessel in the Prince's fleet it suited the dignity of the Royal Heir and was large enough to accommodate the increasing number of people the Count had been forced to include in the party. The wind from the north was fresh and ideal for sailing, and he had co-opted the Prince's best team of oarsmen to add to the power and manoeuvrability of the boat. Apart from the rowers, the crew had been reduced to a minimum to keep the vessel as light as possible. The boat master and steersman were the only senior officers on board. Two sail and rigging men would be helped by the oarsmen when required. The cabin was large, taking up the greater part of the afterdeck. The Count had arranged to have it partitioned to provide private quarters for the Prince and some shelter for the other passengers who had no part in the running of the ship.

Khaemwase's household steward had been horrified to hear from Sunero that his master was to go on such a journey. He was more horrified still to hear the details of the arrangements for the Prince's comfort. 'My Lord never travels with fewer than a dozen servants and then only when going about Mennefer on the King's business. Such a voyage of state requires careful management, planning, and consideration for the Prince's rank. Appearances are everything.'

'Oh, come now, Montmose, since when has His Highness been that worried about appearances? Besides, this isn't a voyage of state but a private visit with no ceremony attached. We'll be there and back before you know it. The Prince has ordered it so.'

'That's as maybe, but what am I to tell the King?'

Suncro grew angry. 'It is not your place to tell the King anything unless you are asked. You are Khaemwase's man. Your duty is to him and if he wants to go to Waset, it is not up to you to ask why. I shall be going with him, and the Count and his wife. Who else do we need to take along, remembering we want to keep the numbers down to the bare minimum?'

They had started to haggle like stall-holders in the market place. Sunero had been able to beat Montmose down to an entourage of four; a body servant, a secretary, a cook and Khaemwase's personal physician. The Steward had gone away grumbling unhappily, but he had fulfilled his side of the bargain by insuring that the chosen servants were provided with all the necessary gear and that they arrived at the boat on time. Each was allocated his tiny space in the cabin area and three of them quickly settled down to make themselves as inconspicuous as possible. The cook, however, insisted on checking all the supplies that the Count had procured and had some very pointed things to say about the lack of forward planning as to menus. Sunero had to stifle a laugh as he watched the already harassed Count enduring the tongue-lashing administered by the cook. The chef's tirade was only halted by the arrival of the Prince himself.

Khaemwase arrived as the sun was clearing the horizon and the city was just beginning to stir. He was brought down to the quayside in a litter and following close behind him came Takhepa in a carrying chair. She alighted first and hurried forward to assist the Prince who, even to Sunero's eyes, was looking pale and weak. The Spy wondered whether this was merely as a result of a sleepless night in anticipation of the voyage, or evidence of some more serious ailment. Takhepa looked genuinely concerned. She had not seen the Prince for years except at a distance. She was shocked to see how much he had changed. To her, he appeared shrunken, bowed, hollow-cheeked. Since Sunero had been in his company almost daily for the last fifteen years or so, he had not noticed the gradual decline which, to Takhepa, appeared as a dramatic and worrying change.

The Count welcomed them all aboard with a cheerfulness which seemed out of place in that pale dawn. He offered his hand to Takhepa to help her up the gangplank but she pushed it away and said something under her breath which only he heard. Sunero saw him frown. Takhepa would always have the last word.

Within moments the ropes were cast off and the oarsmen manoeuvred the boat out into midstream. As the sail was being raised there was a commotion on shore which drew the attention of all on the vessel. A fancy chariot drawn by two high-mettled white horses had clattered down to the end of the quay. The driver was waving his hand to attract attention but had trouble controlling his team and signalling at the same time. Runners quickly followed and words were shouted towards the Prince's boat but none could be made out above the creaking of the spars and the grunting effort of the sailors.

'Ignore him,' Khaemwase said calmly, 'I am retiring to my cabin. I have some sleep to catch up on. Do not disturb me until this evening.' He turned and, supported by his doctor and manservant, he disappeared into the cabin.

Takhepa was still gazing at the shore. 'Who is it?' she asked.

'His son's son,' the Count said before turning his attention to the stowing of baggage. Takhepa turned questioning eyes to Sunero.

'I think our Prince is running away from home,' the Spy said with a wry grin. 'I don't think he told anyone he was going on this trip. The King will not be pleased.'

'What could he do?' Takhepa asked, pointing to the helpless figure of the young man who was now struggling to keep his horses away from the water's edge. The early morning sun glinted off the gold trappings of the chariot harness and from the driver's jewellery. There was a flash of golden light reflecting off an ornate whip as the young nobleman beat it in frustration against the body of the vehicle. The noise, which could not be heard by those on the boat, startled the horses and the young man had to turn his attention to calming the animals before they upset him into the river. The moment had been lost. The Prince had escaped.

Sunero shrugged. 'It looks as if he can do very little now. He could follow us, I suppose, but first I think he will report to his father who will feel obliged to inform the King.'

'What then?'

'I won't even try to predict what the King might do, but I wouldn't be surprised if it was something dramatic. The Prince will have some explaining to do, at some time, but not just now.'

The Count came to stand between them as they watched the outskirts of Mennefer slipping past. 'There will be no story-telling today,' he said, 'so let's sit back and enjoy the ride.' They found the least uncomfortable place to sit amongst the usual ship's deck clutter of coiled ropes and sacking. Sunero and the Count pointed out some of the great monuments which they had visited with the Prince, the pyramids and temples of kings long-dead. It passed a little time but soon there was nothing to do and nothing to say. Sunero found himself half dozing in the warming sun. Takhepa fixed her gaze on the middle distance, lost in her own thoughts. The Count lay back, his hands clasped behind his head, looking with undisguised admiration at his wife. He was remembering the first time he had seen her.

*

When Takhepa had arrived in Egypt, young and a virgin, in the train of the Hittite princess, she had intrigued Khaemwase with her foreign beauty and unsophisticated ways. It pleased Khaemwase to teach Takhepa the arts of love and, at the same time, to explore her mind. He had quickly realised that, as the girl became a woman, she deserved more than to be the plaything of a prince, to be tossed aside when he had wearied of her or when another beauty caught his eye. He had stimulated Takhepa's intellect, her imagination and her awareness of herself and, in doing so, he had revealed to her more aspects of his personality than even his closest family were allowed to see. She could never go back to being a simple servant girl. When the novelty of youth wore off and Khaemwase wanted something more to match his age and experience, he could not abandon her out of hand. Takhepa was his creation, and there was no one else in the world who could truly appreciate such a marvel.

Takhepa had come to Waset in the Prince's entourage when he accompanied the King on the Blessing of Ptah. The honeymoon period of their relationship was long over but Khaemwase would not leave her to the jealousies and enduring rivalries of his harem in Mennefer. He had had the idea to establish her as a housekeeper in the villa on his estate to the south of Waset but even the Prince knew she deserved more of him than to be retired to the country as an old maid at seventeen. When he heard from Sunero of Menhet's establishment and the brothel-keeper's supposed involvement in the Treasury thefts, Khaemwase had seen a way to give Takhepa her freedom and yet serve his own purposes. He was given the idea when he heard Hatiay's report on the two girls who had been placed in Menhet's house as spies. Their information had been of some use but it was not as successful a ploy as Hatiay had hoped. Neither of the girls had caught Siamun's attention and their spying had been restricted to observation of Menhet and the visitors she received. They had given Hatiay several names of merchants who could well have been part of the exchange mechanism for conversion of the stolen goods but the Scribe had been convinced that none of these worthy gentlemen knew the slightest thing about the brothers' clandestine activities even if they were acquainted with either Siamun or Haremheb, which was rarely the case.

Hatiay and Sunero were equally sure that Menhet knew, or chose to know, nothing about the origin of Siamun's wealth. When the King had put a time limit on his son's investigations, he had made everyone think again about the situation. Since Menhet's girls were exclusively foreign, Takhepa's appearance among them would not set tongues wagging. Despite the fact that she was a servant and thus bound to obey her master's commands whatever they might be, Takhepa was given the choice of refusing this task. Khaemwase was not so heartless that he would consign his recent favourite, someone under his protection, to the life of a mindless sex object. He did not want her to feel compelled to do anything unless she freely chose to do it. He explained to her carefully what her situation would be and Hatiay's two girls were brought in to coach her as to what was expected of Menhet's Young Ladies. Together they hatched a plan which would enable Takhepa to avoid becoming simply one high-class foreign whore amongst others. Khaemwase considered their plans carefully and could see little wrong with their reasoning, or so he told himself. Later, when Takhepa had left the safety of his house for the unknown dangers of Waset, he worried that he might have asked too much of her, and that she had been too loyal to refuse him. But his worries soon passed as other more important matters claimed his attention. Just occasionally, in the dark hours of the night, he would wake believing Takhepa to be in his bed beside him and would feel a pang of conscience when he realised the truth. Despite all the reassurances and Takhepa's words of understanding, what sort of man was he if he could so casually send away his one-time lover to become a prostitute?

Takhepa had not been seen in the Prince's entourage before Khaemwase contrived to have her introduced into Menhet's House of Delights, enabling this to be achieved without the connection being made with either the Prince himself or Hatiay. Menhet found her to be a proud but undoubtedly lovely girl who knew her own mind and who was not to be rushed into forming alliances. Her beauty alone began to draw men to the house, each holding the hope that he might prove to be the first of Takhepa's lovers and, as long as the girl was being courted by several hopeful gentlemen, Menhet would not force her to choose any one of them above the others. As the conspirators had hoped, the visitors to Menhet's House were soon engaged in a sort of competition and every participant spent lavishly on gifts for Takhepa, and for the brothel-keeper herself, in the belief that the madame might have some influence over Takhepa's eventual choice. Menhet knew that, once the choice was made, the competition would be over and Takhepa would be no more than an ordinary harlot. She was quite content to leave well enough alone and the Hittite girl was grateful for Menhet's non-interference.

Siamun saw Takhepa for the first time on the night after Sunero's wedding. Still uneasy about allowing the Prince's Man into his family, he had planned to blot out his worries with drink and a woman. He knew that a new girl had joined Menhet's establishment but nothing of what he had heard prepared him for his first glimpse of her. When he entered the main association room, he found it had been reorganised since his last visit. One corner had been curtained off with gauzy linen drapes and within this private area Takhepa was accustomed to hold court, reclining gracefully on a couch, or seated regally on a fine, carved chair, or sprawled casually over a tumble of cushions, while her suitors gathered around, seeing to her every want and waiting for a chance to impress her with the wit of their conversation. It was already clear, to anyone who had met Takhepa, that coarse jokes and innuendo were not to her taste. She was in a different class altogether from the rest of Menhet's girls.

This evening, Takhepa had chosen a chair, and four would-be lovers sat on stools at her feet, ardently pressing their suit in what had become the approved fashion. Her dress was a demure, fringed gown of Asiatic style. Menhet always encouraged her Young Ladies to maintain their foreign allure in the manner of their costume and cosmetics, but Takhepa wore only a hint of blusher on her pale cheeks. Her amber eyes sparkled in the lamplight. Her brown hair shone with highlights of auburn showing that it was not a wig. The only jewellery she wore was a plain golden chain with a pendant representing the Syrian goddess Anath. This had been a parting gift from Khaemwase, but no one would learn that from her, just as no one, not even Menhet herself, knew that Takhepa was a Hittite. She had let it be known that she came from 'the far north', which was true enough, and she was quite content when Menhet's clients interpreted this as 'Syria'. The only other 'Syrian' girl in the house had been born in Egypt of mixed parentage and could not hold the most basic of conversations in her 'mother tongue' whereas Takhepa, having soaked up all that Khaemwase could teach her, was a gifted linguist. The virginal simplicity of her dress and the plainness of her make-up, her elegant bearing and her natural charm, all served to set her apart from the gaudily painted, heavily scented and scantily dressed whores who entertained their clients in the same room. Siamun could only gaze at her in disbelief.

The old madame, her hennaed hair even brighter since Takhepa's arrival in an attempt to mimic the younger girl's fairer colouring, took Siamun to one side and handed him a brimming wine cup, saying, 'She's not like the rest, lad. You won't be able to jump her like you can Tjesia or Hethma. You'll have to make her want you.'

Siamun, his eyes dazzled by Takhepa's beauty before she had cast even a single glance in his direction, had a sudden vision of the future, his future, and Takhepa was part of it. He had never wanted to commit himself to a sole being and yet, one sight of this unknown and, as far as anyone knew, unreachable lovely, had quite turned his head. Siamun was in love. He spent the night drinking slowly and watching her from a distance. On that occasion she made no sign that she had even noticed his existence. When she rose to bid her companions good night, Siamun joined the courtiers whose hopes had been dashed, as they began some serious drinking. All the while she chose to favour no one in particular, there was no jealousy and no bad feeling. They were all kindred spirits, linked in their quest of the unattainable. Considering how Takhepa might be seen to be leading them on, there was a notable lack of resentment towards her. A single word out of place and the mouth that uttered it would have been silenced by several fists. Meanwhile, they drank together as companions drowning their shared disappointments and comparing their thoughts and hopes about the object of their desire.

So, Siamun fell in love and at the same time sowed the seeds of his own destruction. But even knowing what they knew now, neither Sunero nor Takhepa doubted that Siamun would have acted differently. Siamun could no more not have fallen for Takhepa than fly in the air. Love makes fools of everyone.

*

Travelling by day, the river's banks slipped by quickly with the constant wind from the north keeping the sail billowed. Siamun and Sunero were frustrated by the demand of the Prince's chef that the ship's master made at least two stops each day in order to take on fresh supplies of bread, beer and garden produce, or to fish. The chef and the ship's cook had come to an amicable arrangement over the use of the portable stoves to prepare simple but ample meals for the passengers on board. Cooking for the crew had to be done over fires on shore, necessitating further delays to their southward progress. At dusk the boat's captain directed the rowers to take the vessel to a safe mooring for the night.

'I shall be putting on weight with all this food and no exercise,' the Count complained. Takhepa, nibbling daintily at a duck carcase, snorted, 'What makes you think you're such a perfect figure anyway? Have you really looked at yourself lately?'

The Count looked hurt and spent some while contemplating his stomach before replying, 'Are you saying I'm fat?'

Takhepa grinned mischievously, 'I'm not saying anything, but if the peg fits the hole...' She let that thought fester.

The Count turned to Sunero, 'Do you think I'm fat?'

'I'm not taking sides between husband and wife,' he said. Privately he mused, '*He has let himself go recently. I remember the time when he was slim and bronzed, with powerful shoulders that could lift huge blocks of stone without a second thought. But that was all of twenty years ago. He's nearly forty-five now, and I'm past fifty. Life has a poor sense of humour.*'

To everyone's surprise, and not a little dismay, they had been three full days into the voyage before the Prince called them together to continue the story. On the morning of the fourth day, he drew back the reed curtain of his cabin and emerged to sit in the shade of the awning, indicating that the Spy, the Count and Takhepa should join him. 'Have you had enough time to bring your stories to agreement?' he asked.

Sunero was still not certain whether his Lord was joking, but Takhepa, in her irreverent way, said, 'There's no need for that. We all remember well enough without having to check each other's story.'

'Well, let us see where we can start. I think Sunero had just brought me to the point where I had to take a hand in the matter to speed things along. Perhaps it is up to me to begin.' Without mentioning the King's ultimatum, Khaemwase began to explain, for the first time, what he had done.

*

The Prince had summoned Harmose and had put the fear of Seth into him. 'These thefts cannot much longer remain a secret from His Majesty,' he said to the Custodian. 'Should the King discover the truth, whose head do you think he will want? Not mine, you can be sure.'

Harmose stammered something unintelligible but heavy with fear. Khaemwase continued, 'We need a trap, Harmose. We must catch these thieves in the act. As you have not yet discovered how they get into the Treasury, you must set a trap inside. Can you do that?'

Harmose had been giving serious thought to that very problem. 'I can't leave guards inside every night, Highness. We never know when the raiders will strike next and Your Highness wouldn't want me to give my men the opportunity to go poking around in His Majesty's private belongings, which is what they would do out of sheer boredom after a while. But with Your Highness' permission, I think I could set a sort of deadfall trap.'

'Do you mean the sort of trap that could injure or even kill the victim?'

'Yes, Highness. I think that's the only sort that will work. We'll never catch them by waiting for them to make another mistake. They've already proved they're as cunning as foxes so we'll treat them like animals and set them an animal trap.'

'And how will this trap work '

Harmose explained. 'So you see, Your Highness, I must have your permission to make the necessary alterations.'

'You have it, Harmose. And do it soon, I grow impatient to have the rogues caught. You must be careful how you choose your workmen. We can be sure of no one at present. May I suggest that you find the men you need from the East Bank workshops rather than here at the

Mansion, and blindfold them so that they do not know where they are going. And finally, there is no need to tell Sunero of this. I shall tell him, in my own time.'

*

Sunero grunted softly, but the Prince's sharp ears heard him nevertheless. 'Yes, Sunero, I know my own time has been long in coming, but I had some doubt still about your loyalties. Harmose was unaware of our suspicions as to the perpetrators of the crime. You had become so involved that I knew you would not approve of such drastic measures. However, as you know, I had my own reasons for bringing this nagging problem to an end. Harmose's plan seemed to be a way out, for all of us.'

'Did you think, Lord, that I would have warned them if I had known about Harmose's trap?' Sunero asked in a hurt tone.

'Would you have done so?' the Prince turned the question back on the Spy. Sunero hung his head. He could not answer. He had often wondered about this, particularly on dark, sleepless nights, and when he remembered Baketi. Could he honestly swear that he would have kept silent at the Prince's command and let her brothers walk into a potentially lethal trap? No one could answer that. It was too late now.

'And then, of course, there was the second part of my plan,' the Prince said quickly, to cover Sunero's embarrassment. He held out his hand to Takhepa who came to kneel by his side. 'Yes, my dear. We had had our time together, a time I shall never forget, but tastes change and we both knew that it could not last. I did not do too badly by you, did I? You have no regrets?'

'No, Lord,' she answered softly. 'Without knowing it, you put me in the way of finding my greatest happiness. How can I regret that?'

'At least, it seems, I did not do everything wrong,' Khaemwase smiled a rare smile, 'but it was Sunero's idea really.' Sunero prepared to deny this but the Prince went on, 'He told me how my local agent, Hatiay, had placed two girls in Menhet's House of Delights. It was a good idea, but they were mere servant girls and the task called for intelligence and beauty. Who better than my sweet Takhepa to fill that position?' For a while there was an easy silence as each drifted into his or her own memories of that time.

Takhepa, with a girlish smile playing on her lips, remembered some of the many excuses she had used for rejecting almost every eligible young man in Waset. She could see their earnest faces still, and recall their names, names which, had she been less scrupulous, she could have used to great advantage. What would a rich man pay to keep from his wife the fact that he was lusting after a foreign chit of a girl? Takhepa could have made her fortune several times over.

The Count remembered his first tongue-tied approach to the glorious amber-eyed beauty who had bewitched him at a glance. He recalled her first smile which had set his blood coursing like liquid fire. He remembered the envious muttering of the other suitors who had seen the newcomer to their ranks so favoured on his first introduction.

Sunero was out of touch with events. He had not visited Menhet's establishment since that first night with Siamun. Once he was married to Siamun's sister, he could hardly risk being seen by her brother, blatantly deceiving his new wife. He had not been told about Takhepa and, although the news of Menhet's latest acquisition spread quickly about the city, he did not associate the Syrian Queen, as she came to be known, with the Prince's Hittite dalliance.

Khaemwase watched the emotions flitting across the faces of those he now recognised as his closest friends. He had been the instrument of their greatest achievements as well as their greatest disappointments. He held their lives in his hand. In the Count's case, he could have snuffed out that life with a word. What had been gained by their association? Had it all been for his amusement and nothing more? He had to believe that his interference in their lives had been justified and that something good had come of it, though interference it had been, and whether their lives would have been any better without his manipulation only the gods knew. Soon, very soon, Khaemwase would have to justify his actions before the supreme Judge. There, in the Hall of Osiris, he would explain how he had spun, woven, unravelled and reworked these threads of existence to his own designs. Any snags in the thread, any flaws in the weave, were his mistakes. The threads themselves had no power to influence the final pattern. They were his responsibility and, like Wepwawet, the Opener of Ways, he would prepare the path for them, smoothing their passage to the Afterlife as best he could.

Chapter Ten

The boat continued on the southward journey, the creaking of the spars under the tension of the sail and ropes, and the rhythmic splash of the oars providing a constant background of noise, augmented at times by the shouts and conversations of the crew and some more distant sounds from the riverbanks. They were making good speed in spite of the regular stops for meals and replenishment of stores. Sunero found it all too easy to become mesmerised by the patterns of light flickering on the rippling water. He realised that all his companions were similarly lost in contemplation of the infinite. How peaceful, how relaxing it was, as if time meant nothing. While they stayed within the neutrality of the river's midstream, they were no part of the life of Kemet. They were detached, neither entering into the thoughts of those on shore nor wishing to be included in those thoughts. Sunero could almost believe that, if they stayed on the boat forever, they would all remain exactly as they were now, never aging, never failing, never dying. Perhaps the Count was right. Perhaps this was just what the Prince needed, a pause in his hectic life, giving him time to think, to put things into perspective. But then the Spy knew the Prince better than that.

As the raucous sound of a braying donkey in the distance brought him back to reality, Sunero knew beyond question that Khaemwase was dying, and that nothing anyone could do now would halt that process. It would be when the Prince thought the time was right and in a place he considered to be suitably auspicious, but it would be. And it would be soon. The Prince's death was as inevitable as the sunrise. Neither Sunero nor the Count had ever had the slightest influence over Khaemwase's decision. Earlier in their storytelling the Count had likened their actions to those of a fisherman playing a lively fish, but now the Spy realised their roles had been reversed. Khaemwase held the fishing rod. He had let them think that they were tugging him in the direction they wished to take when, in fact, he was inexorably drawing them towards his chosen landing place. The Count may still believe that this trip to Waset was his idea but Sunero now understood the truth. It had always been the Prince's intention to go to the Holy City. He had manipulated them, used everyone to his own ends, just as he had always done.

The security of their private musings was interrupted by the Prince's physician who insisted that his patient should rest in the cabin during the midday heat. To Sunero's surprise, Khaemwase allowed himself to be led away like a docile child. This, perhaps more than anything, convinced the Spy of his master's decline. He never would have consented to such bullying in his prime. The sun was high and the air clear. The breeze, which kept the boat moving southwards, was pleasant, but the day was hot and soon all but the on-watch rowers and the steersman were dozing in what little shade could be found. Sunero fell asleep and dreamed of Baketamen for the first time in a long while.

*

Baketi had been a better wife than Sunero deserved. Like her mother, she was practical and resourceful. She was an excellent cook, when given the opportunity to demonstrate her skill, and her sewing was praised by all. Indeed, friends and neighbours brought all sorts of needlework for Baketi to do because her stitches were so fine and neat. Living at first with Haremheb and Meryt, the newlyweds had found life very easy. Merytamen had refused to let Baketi help in the kitchen, saying there were servants as well as herself and Tiye to do the work. However, when Meryt became ill, she was very glad for Baketi to take over the running of the household.

Sunero spent much of his time with Hatiay as the Prince had found him estate work to do and this took him, more often than not, out of the City. He had not even been able to identify which of the brothers had the scarred foot and that annoyed him. He had been so proud of noticing that small but crucial piece of evidence, and yet he had been unable to make any further progress. Siamun usually wore sandals at work where he was constantly walking over irregular surfaces strewn with sharp stone chippings. Sunero rarely saw him during daylight hours and, since they were living in different houses, they met only occasionally in the evening when, in the dim lamplight, nothing but the closest examination would have told him what he wanted to know. The Spy could hardly demand to see either brother's left heel without a reasonable excuse. Even living at close quarters with Haremheb made Sunero's investigation no easier. The opportunity to examine Hari's foot never presented itself and the women were so house-proud that Sunero had no chance to study his footprints on the floor. The Spy found that his only means of positively identifying at least one of the thieves was, as yet, unusable.

During this time of frustration and lack of progress, Baketamen was a constant source of strength and comfort. As he watched her helping Meryt look after little Simut, and teaching Tiye her stitches, he found he valued her company and was proud of her achievements. When he found that he had begun to think of her as 'my wife' instead of 'Siamun's sister', he knew that he truly cared for her. Love came later, perhaps too late. Meryt's tragic death brought about a number of changes in the two households. Simut was taken in by Rai as she considered Tiye too young to be given the responsibility of mothering the child. Hari, too, moved back to his mother's home. He could not face life alone in the house full of such bitter-sweet memories. Within the shortest possible time, Tiye was married off to a young trainee clerk from Hari's department, leaving Sunero and Baketi as sole occupants of the older Simut's house.

The Spy took the earliest opportunity to examine the house from cellar to roof to see if anything might come to light to prove his suspicions, but the brothers, as their father and his brother before them, had been far wiser than to keep incriminating evidence in their own homes. When Sunero investigated the storeroom, he too failed to notice the mismatch between internal and external measurements. When, later, he found out about the secret room, he could have kicked himself for missing something so obvious. He carried out a thorough inventory of the stores he knew about and ruthlessly threw out a lot of rubbish so that he could see exactly what and where everything was. It was much the same exercise, though on a smaller scale, that Harmose had conducted in the Treasury. Then, all he could do was wait.

Baketi waited too, waited patiently and longingly for a child. Sunero knew what she wanted but he was not prepared to add that complication to his life. He felt desperately sorry for Baketamen, who anxiously counted the days of her cycle and fell into a fit of depression each time her moonflow started, proving yet again that she was not pregnant. Soon Rai would be asking questions of her daughter as to why she had not done her duty as a wife. Baketi's elder sister Nefertari, after all, had produced a child every year of her marriage so far, and her cousin Nofret had been pregnant twice, though the first child had miscarried. Even Tiye was expecting. There was clearly nothing wrong with the female side of the family, but Baketi was loyal. She would never put the blame on her husband and he had no wish to see her branded as barren. If only matters could be settled quickly. If he could take Baketamen away from Waset, set up a home in Mennefer, far away from sight and sound of her family, then things would be different. Meanwhile, Sunero told himself that a family was the last thing he wanted. He had to keep his mind on the job in hand. The treasury thefts must be dealt with and a final seal put on the case. It had dragged on for far too long. It was more than six years since Takhenet's trial.

*

Several days passed before the Prince was ready to talk again, further confirming Sunero's belief that his master was nearing his end. When Khaemwase called them together again, they had passed Abdu and turned eastwards into the great bend of the river. The rowers were working harder now, with the wind coming across the ship's bow, and their speed had slowed to a more leisurely pace. With the major part of the voyage behind him, the Prince clearly felt it was time to tie up loose ends.

'Tell me, Count,' he said, 'about that last raid.'

It was no less than a royal command. The Count had to obey no matter how painful it might be. With Meryt's funeral, the family's fortunes suffered another blow, and Tiye's marriage also depleted the stores though her dowry had been modest enough. For a while Hari was in no state even to consider a visit to the Treasury but eventually, as his sorrow gave way in some part to anger, it was easy for Siamun to convince him that another raid would be some sort of revenge for Meryt's death. They entered the Treasury by their usual route although this time they had no clear plan as to what they would take. Siamun wanted to shake Haremheb out of his grief.

'See,' he said, 'see what the King has! He won't miss what little we take and yet think what a difference even that little makes to us.' He ran his hands over a bale of soft, white linen. 'Think what we could do with this. Think how you could provide for little Simut's future. He may be motherless but he need never be poor.'

Hari nodded. He had suffered a dreadful blow but he had to recover for his son's sake. For a while it was unthinkable that Meryt could be replaced but, in time, he would remarry and make a new home for his son. However, to do that properly, he would take whatever he wanted. He looked around the middle hall where all the choice wines and perfumes were stored. He estimated the degree of wealth represented by a single jar. 'Why do we bother with these heavy things?' he asked his brother sharply. 'Why break our backs only to give ourselves the further trouble of disguising the stuff to get rid of it? Why don't we just take the gold?'

The Count's voice faltered in his telling of the tale. He said, 'I couldn't argue with him. We'd already taken some of the really valuable stuff, against all that our father had advised. Taking more seemed so easy and Hari was in no mood to be thwarted. I didn't even try to stop him.' He broke down and it was some moments before he was calm enough to continue. 'Hari went to the doors into the gold room. The right one was closed and the left one was just a little ajar. They're heavy things and Hari knew how much effort it took to open them. He put both hands to the door's edge and pulled but it stuck. That just made him angry so he put all his strength to it and pulled again. This time the door moved but it twisted and fell. The whole thing came away from its sockets and fell on Hari.'

The Count now had tears falling freely down his cheeks but he felt compelled to tell all. 'It fell across him as it twisted and he was crushed to the floor with that huge, bronze-plated slab of wood pinning him from the waist down. He screamed, and the noise of the falling door and Hari's voice seemed to echo around the Treasury forever. I couldn't believe that no one else would have heard it but no one came and, when the echoes finally died away, there was Hari, half-conscious, trapped! I stood there, helpless, just like when Father died. It was as if my memory of that time, the memory that had haunted my dreams for years, had been made real. Instead of Father lying beneath the stone there was Hari under the metal-clad door. The door was so heavy I couldn't possibly lift it on my own, but I tried just as I had tried to lift the stela from Father. What else could I do? Even with levers, one man couldn't have done anything. Then I saw the blood. The door had crushed Hari's legs and one of his thigh bones had been pushed through the flesh. He was bleeding badly. He was bleeding to death, and I could do nothing. I couldn't staunch the blood because I couldn't even reach the wound. I had to sit and watch him die.

'Hari came to for a short while and seemed perfectly coherent. He said, "You must leave me here. Go! Don't let them catch you too." But I couldn't do that. I said nothing but he insisted, "Promise me! You must leave. Someone has to look after Simut and Mother!" I knew he was right but I still couldn't leave while he was alive. Then he said, "They'll recognise me when they find me. That will lead them to you. You must protect the family. Take my head!" I couldn't believe what he was saying. I was horrified, but he persisted. "It's the only way. Take my head then they'll only find an anonymous body and if you seal up the entrance properly, no one will ever know." How could I do it? I knew he was right, but how could I take my own brother's head? For a while he lay still and then, quite suddenly, he grabbed my hand and said, "Promise me, Siamun, don't let them identify me, for Simut's sake." I had to promise. I had to promise! Then he died.'

The story had its own momentum now and nothing would stop it. The Count continued, 'I went back to the first hall, and found a chest of woodworking tools. I took a saw and a knife. I found a basket and some rags. I cut off my brother's head. I wrapped it in linen and packed it in the basket, before going out by our usual route. I took nothing else that time and I never went back. I went down to the river to wash off my brother's blood, then I sat on the bank until near dawn, wondering what I was going to tell the family. As the sun rose, the full horror of what had happened struck me and I wept. I have never wept so hard nor so long, before or since. Suddenly it hit me that, within the space of little more than a year, we had lost my father, my brother had lost his wife and now I had lost my brother. It seemed as if the gods were punishing me. I felt dreadfully alone and I didn't know what to do, so I wept for them and for myself.'

When the Count fell silent, it was as if the world had stopped. Momentarily, there was no sound, no movement, no one even drew breath. Then the moment had passed and the Count sobbed. Takhepa moved to his side and put her arms about him. He fell on her shoulder and wept again. The Prince waved his dismissal and the meeting was over. Sunero could have sworn that there were tears in his master's eyes.

*

The blood was still wet, a dark, glistening pool in which the pale, headless body lay like a sandbar emerging from the river in summer. The door lay where it had fallen and on top of it were the blood-stained tools, eloquent evidence of the gruesome task for which they had been employed. Sunero felt sick. He swallowed hard, again and again, before whispering hoarsely, 'What happened?'

Harmose told him how he had brought in a carpenter to saw almost completely through the pivots on one of the door flaps on the entrance to the metal store. The weight of the door held it upright so that, to all outward appearances it was undamaged but pulling on the door destroyed that delicate balance causing the pivots to break, springing Harmose's trap.

The Custodian was almost glowing with pride. 'My trap worked. There is our thief.'

Sunero found himself fighting back another bout of nausea brought on by Harmose's obvious pleasure in the bloody sight. Softly, but with barely restrained anger, the Spy said, 'You fool, Harmose! Look again. We have a body, but that proves nothing except that at least one other thief escaped your heavy-handed scheme. '

The Custodian looked hurt, and then puzzled, 'How?'

'By all the gods, man, who do you think cut off the head? Have you found it? No! Then the man who cut it off took it away with him. What evidence is left? A faceless, unidentifiable body!'

Harmose's brow creased in serious thought. Sunero was spoiling the elation he had felt at the success of his plan, but now he saw that all he had learned about the robbers was that one of them would never steal again. He tried to see this as a positive outcome of his plan, saying, 'Perhaps we have put an end to the pillaging of His Majesty's stores. At least that is something.'

'But we don't know who they are,' Sunero was conscious of the hypocrisy in his baiting of Harmose. He was angry that the matter had been taken out of his hands, furious that the painstaking work of Hatiay and his team should be so dramatically and pointlessly curtailed. Most of all, he was cut to the heart that one of the brothers now lay dead at his feet and he knew he was to blame. But which of the brothers was it? He forced himself to study the body, or what he could see of it. Clearly, the torso had not the muscular shoulders of the stonemason. It had to be Hari. Sunero bent forward to lift the right hand. The palm and fingertips were covered in blood but, even in the flickering lamplight, he could see that the hand bore no calluses except for an ink-blackened thickening on the middle finger. A scribe. It was Haremheb. He placed the hand gently back on the floor.

The Custodian had been watching him closely, 'You know him don't you? You've known all the time.' Anger began to rise in Harmose's voice, 'You won't tell me, even now, after everything. You never meant for me to find out, did you? Well, I have my orders and I intend to follow them.' He turned his back on the Spy and summoned workmen, who had been standing by with levers and wedges, to come and raise the door. 'We'll see how his accomplices like the idea of his body being hung on the town wall.'

Sunero could hold back his nausea no longer. He rushed from the Treasury and just managed to reach the side gate before he was violently sick.

*

'A nasty predicament,' Khaemwase drawled, with little emotion in his voice. His momentary display of humanity had passed. He was, as ever, in total command of his feelings to the extent of appearing cold and indifferent. 'Now, tell me, Count, how you explained your brother's disappearance to your mother.'

The Count took a deep breath. The Prince knew that this would be the most difficult and hurtful part of the story but he insisted on having every detail. There was no escape.

*

Siamun had sat on the riverbank, the unremarkable lidded basket by his side, until the first flight of waterfowl from the reedbeds announced the dawn. After grief and guilt had racked his body with sobs so deep they seemed to tear at his heart, he had had time to think. Always quick to see the way through a problem, always first to come up with a plan, he had spent half the night in blank despair with not a single idea as to how he could explain Hari's loss without revealing everything. The rest of the family would take his brother's death as disaster enough without Siamun bringing shame and ruin on them too. His mother would have to be told something believable, she was no fool, but he could not bring himself to break faith with his father's spirit. Amenhotep had managed to keep Rai in ignorance of the Secret throughout their very successful marriage, so Siamun would not destroy his father's memory even though it meant incriminating himself in another, lesser crime.

Tomb robbery had always been an occupation, if not a profession, of the middle classes in Waset. Everyone knew someone else who was involved. Rai would have to acknowledge that the recent drains on the family's resources in the way of dowries and funeral expenses could not have been supported solely by the incomes of the two brothers. He would tell his mother that they had had to turn to tomb robbery and Hari had been trapped by a rock-fall, a well-known hazard of the trade. Rai would understand.

Rai understood. She wept and she wailed, and she tore her hair and beat her breast. She cursed Siamun for leading Haremheb astray, for she naturally assumed that the older brother was the instigator of the scheme. She cursed the gods for their cruelty in the sequence of events that had driven her sons to such desperate measures. She cursed the authorities for paying such meagre wages that her children should risk their lives to enable their family to live in modest comfort. She tenderly unwrapped Haremheb's head and stroked the bloodied cheeks. Then there was a long, painful silence. Rai spoke first, 'How can we bury him without his body?'

This had been puzzling Siamun too. No embalmer would keep quiet, whatever the inducement, if asked to prepare only a severed head for burial.

'It's always possible to find a body,' Siamun said, knowing as he said it that this was an unacceptable solution.

'He cannot go before Osiris with a borrowed body. How can the Judges assess his worthiness if the heart they weigh is not his? You must fetch his body. Find others to help you. Dig him out. Bring him home.'

Siamun dared not argue though, at the time, he had no idea how he could retrieve his brother's corpse. He toyed with the idea of re-entering the Treasury so that, although he could not remove Hari's body, he could bring back the all-important heart, but deep down he knew that was impossible. He could never return to the Treasury, the Secret would never be used again.

*

The Spy was the first to speak. 'Harmose played right into your hands. He was so sure he was outsmarting you by taking the body out of the Treasury that he did all the hard work for you.'

The Count grinned, a humourless grin. The most painful part was over, he had hardened his heart again. He could now detach himself from events so far in the past. He had learned to do so, many years ago. It was the only way to stop the pain. The boat glided along the timeless river which would eventually wash away all sins, all pain, leaving everything pure and acceptable. The story-telling was a form of purification. The voyage now coming to its end was the journey to acceptance.

The Prince did not call them together again until early on the morning of the day when they expected to dock at Waset. He was eager to draw together all the loose threads before they stepped on shore. Sunero took up the tale.

*

He had reacted to Harmose's summons just as Siamun was returning with his terrible news. It was with great difficulty that the Spy schooled his thoughts to return home knowing, but not supposed to know, that his wife's brother was dead. Baketi greeted him with tears and the story that Siamun had told his mother. Sunero had to show shock, horror, anger, all the emotions expected at the news of such a bereavement and the revelation of the criminal dealings of the two brothers. What he felt, most acutely, was a grudging respect for the mind that had concocted such a plausible story to cover the real crime. Siamun would not want to see him. Baketamen was begging him to keep the family's grief a secret, to save her mother further pain. He promised her all she wanted, that was the easy part since he knew it would not be he who revealed her brothers' crimes. Siamun was well on the way to condemning himself without the Spy's further intervention.

The Count took up the story, the words flowing easily now as the end came closer. Within half a day of Sunero having left the Treasury, Harmose had carried out his threat and the body was taken across the River to be hung on the town wall with two temple guards keeping watch for anyone who might show signs of grief at the sight. The news of the latest unusual attraction soon spread and townsfolk flocked to see the headless corpse, some even making a special excursion across from the Western Town, but no one recognised it and speculation was rife as to who it might be. The news of Hari's death was kept a family secret for several days. His absence from work was put down to an attack of fever and no one thought to question the truth of the matter since it was that time of year and the family was still considered to be beyond reproach.

When Rai heard about the 'criminal' corpse on public display, she wept and wailed all over again. There was no doubt in her mind that it was Hari's. How many decapitated bodies were there in Waset? Harmose had stopped short of announcing exactly where the body had been found. It was simply described as being that of a thief who had violated a royal place. This description was interpreted by all as meaning one of the more audacious tomb robbers who worked the royal sepulchres of the Great Place. This convinced Rai that it was her son's body which was being ogled and reviled by all and sundry.

'What are you going to do about it?' she demanded of her elder son. 'You can't let him stay there. You must bring him home.'

By the fourth day, the novelty had worn off. The body was beginning to smell badly and everyone who wanted to see it had seen it. The guards were becoming bored. In the evening, an elderly man appeared leading a sorry-looking, over-laden donkey. As he shambled past, one of the guards noticed something and shouted, 'Hey, mate, one of your skins is leaking.'

The old man stopped and went back to examine his load. Sure enough, there was a steady trickle of dark liquid coming from the neck of one of the skin sacks. He began to curse as he fiddled with the cord tying the neck, but he only seemed to make the leak worse. The guards could smell the drink now. It was wine and a good wine at that, not vinegary but sweet-smelling and fruity.

'Need any help, friend?' the first guard said, stepping forward in the hope that he might get a taste of the fragrant liquor.

'I can't stop the flow,' the donkey man said, 'I won't be able to save even half the skinful by the time I get back to my master.'

'We'll save it for you,' the guard said, with a quick grin and a knowing look towards his partner. 'I hate to see it just soaking into the ground. If you're going to lose it anyway, why not let it go where it'll be appreciated?'

The old man was a little simple and needed it explained to him more than once, but when the guards had finally got the idea across, he was more than willing to join them in 'saving' his master's wine from going to waste. The wine was more potent than the guards expected, but the taste was so fine that they passed the skin back and forth, not noticing that the old man drank only one swallow to their ten. There was still half a skinful left when the second guard at last slumped against the wall, dead to the world. When the relief guards arrived after sunset, they found their companions snoring loudly, and the body gone.

The embalmer was paid very well. He would have been a deaf and blind fool if he had not identified the decomposing, headless corpse as that which had so recently decorated the town wall, but with head and body reunited, the mummy bandages concealed all. It was announced that Hari, sadly, had succumbed to the fever and, if any neighbours or friends put two and two together, they never expressed their suspicions in words. The family had suffered enough.

On the night after the funeral, Siamun paid what he thought was to be his last visit to Menhet's house, He could no longer afford Takhepa's price and this made him doubly miserable. For the first time in ages, he got drunk and, in the darkest part of the early morning, he poured out his heart to his beloved. He was not foolish enough, even in his drunkenness, to mention the Treasury. The tomb-robbing story had been well rehearsed, but he did describe how he had greyed his hair with limestone dust, lined his face with makeup from his mother's dressing box, and disguised his youthful body with a shapeless, ragged wrap-around and a filthy kilt.

'But it was all worth it. He's dead and buried now, properly buried too. I owed him that.' Still not able to bring himself to tell Takhepa that he would not be coming back, he gave her a parting gift of greater magnificence than any previous tribute. It was the last of the goods from the final raid on the Treasury. It was a carnelian plaque of unusual translucence and colour, carved with a sphinx in the Hittite style. It seemed highly appropriate as a gift for his northern beauty, his most beloved, the woman he would never see again.

Chapter Eleven

Everyone sensed the change of mood. They could not help but be affected by what they had heard, but it had been a necessary part of the healing process, like the sharp pain of a lanced boil or the sting of ointment in an open wound. Now the spell was broken. The nightmares had been exorcised. They could breathe again.

The Prince slapped his thigh and laughed, 'Ha! So that was how it ended! How careless of you, my dear Count, and how appropriate that your choice of that particular jewel should give you away. What became of it?'

Takhepa took up the story. She was an intelligent girl and she immediately recognised the jewel as Hittite craftsmanship. She knew the quality and the types of goods which had accompanied her former mistress from their northern homeland and she knew that Sunero had deposited just such goods in the King's Treasury. This was the sort of thing she had been told to look for and to report to Hatiay. Even so, it was some days before she could bring herself to do her duty. Already her feelings for Siamun had become quite bewildering, and she was torn between her loyalty to the Prince and a new, overwhelming experience which she was beginning to identify as love. When it was clear to her that Siamun would not be visiting her again, she felt deserted and betrayed, so it was almost out of spite that she delivered the carnelian plaque to Hatiay's office. The scribe recognised it at once from the description on one of the inventories of stolen goods and could hardly believe his luck. He sent a messenger to find Sunero and, in his jubilation at finding success at last, he also sent a hurriedly drafted note to inform the Prince of the latest development.

'I remember it well,' Khaemwase interrupted. 'The discovery was so conveniently timed. I had arrived in Waset only that morning to prepare for the proclamation of His Majesty's Third Jubilee. Hatiay's note was delivered within moments of his writing it. It was not the most literary of documents. Have you a copy in that box of yours, Sunero?'

'No, My Lord. Hatiay sent it in such haste that he never made a copy.'

'I remember my secretary was most upset about it. He thought the tone was too familiar and was all for having me dismiss Hatiay on the spot, but I recognised the importance of the note by what Hatiay had managed to say without revealing any details. His exultation was obvious in every line, and the feelings simply oozed off the page as if the ink were still wet, which it almost was. By the time I came to read it, which was, I suppose, in the evening of the day it was written, I imagine you, Sunero, had already conferred with Hatiay and made your plans.'

*

Hatiay's messenger to the Spy had caused quite an uproar in the household. He was most insistent that the message could only be delivered into Sunero's hand but the Spy was not at home when the messenger arrived. He had gone, with Baketi's mother, to arrange for her passage to Suan. It had been decided, at last, that Rai should take her youngest child Shery, and little Simut, to live with her married daughter Nefertari. There was nothing to keep her in Waset any longer. Baketi would eventually return to Mennefer with her husband and Siamun showed no signs of ever marrying. All the other children were provided for and it seemed most sensible to dispose of at least one of the properties in Waset to raise some capital so that Rai, and particularly little Simut, could start a comfortable new life away from the scene of so many tragedies. Since the funeral, Siamun seemed to have been either working all the hours possible or to be drinking himself senseless. Without Hari to share his confidences, Siamun felt the weight of the world on his shoulders and the burden of so many secrets was bringing him low. Rai had turned to Sunero as the most responsible member of the family to help her make the arrangements for the move.

When they returned from the dockside, they found Hatiay's messenger camped in the entrance hall. The Scribe had impressed upon him the importance of the prompt delivery of the note and the speedy return of its bearer in the company of Sunero. The messenger thought it was more than his job, and possibly his life, was worth to return alone and with the note undelivered, so he had refused to move until he had carried out his errand. Baketi was flustered, not knowing whether to treat the man as an honoured guest or to despise him for an officious subordinate who was making a drama out of a simple matter of carrying a message. When, at last, Sunero took the note from the man's hand, Baketi was as relieved as the messenger himself, who went to wait outside. Reading the letter, Sunero felt a cold hand about his heart. He had hoped, in his deepest, personal thoughts, that Hari's death would be enough to satisfy the Prince and that the matter was finished. He had prayed, to any god who would listen, that Siamun would give up all ideas of returning to the Treasury, that the thieving would stop, and all evidence of past crimes would be buried, but he had reckoned without love.

By the time the Spy reached Hatiay's office, it was mid-afternoon. The sphinx on the carnelian plaque seemed to stare at him accusingly. There could be no doubt that it was from the Hittite Marriage treasure. How could Siamun have been so stupid?

'Yes,' he said, 'I recognise it. So we have clear evidence now.' Then he paused for a moment's thought. 'But do we, Hatiay? Do we really have proof? He's been clever enough to cover his tracks so far with perfectly plausible stories. Couldn't he just claim that he got it through the black market? The worst we could pin on him would be receiving stolen goods.'

Hatiay's face fell. 'I sent a message to the Prince,' he admitted, 'I was so sure we had it all cleared up.' Both men racked their memories for any clue which could put their case beyond doubt. Then Sunero slapped his palm to his forehead, 'Tracks! Cover his tracks! I didn't look to see if Hari was the one with the scar on his foot. If he was, we're done for. If it's Siamun, then we've won!' But neither Sunero nor Hatiay felt any real sense of victory.

Very shortly after this anticlimactic meeting, the Prince's summons arrived. They were to collect Takhepa and bring her to make her personal report. *It is hoped*, the message continued, *that at last, after all these years of waiting, our little problem will soon be laid to rest.*

*

Khaemwase chuckled, 'A masterpiece of understatement of which I'm quite proud. That meeting was most entertaining. I remember Hatiay trying to be impartial and to put all sides of the case as clearly and concisely as possible. I remember you, Sunero, trying to do your job and, at the same time, find a way out for your wife's brother. And, sweet Takhepa, you were begging for mercy for the wretch you clearly loved and yet whom you had just betrayed. Most entertaining. There was only one thing to be done. I had to see this Siamun for myself.'

*

With great audacity, Sunero had suggested that it might be kinder to leave the arrest until Rai had departed for Suan. The Prince agreed with reluctance. What were a few more days on top of the years already spent in unravelling this mystery? To tell the truth, Sunero was still hoping against hope that he could provide Siamun with a way to avoid what appeared to be an inevitable death sentence. It all depended on the heel of Siamun's left foot, no mention of which had been made to Khaemwase.

Siamun saw his mother, sister and little Simut off at the quayside, promising to send on their share of the proceeds of the property sale. Then he returned home prepared to drink himself into a stupor of forgetfulness, or at least a short respite from the memories which continually haunted his waking and sleeping dreams. Waiting in his hall with Sunero were two of the Prince's guards. He knew, instantly, why they had come for him. He meekly acknowledged Sunero's authority and went without a fuss. He had no time for even one jar of beer.

In the end, Siamun condemned himself. It was such a relief to tell his story, even to find out that other people knew, or suspected, most of the truth already. He repeated the ancient family grievance against Ameneminet, giving his father's explanation of why the Designer's family had felt justified in robbing the King, though bound by his oath he stopped short of revealing the existence of the secret entrance. He explained the family's reasoning behind the taking of certain things and the leaving of others, and he admitted that he had been foolish to step outside the bounds set by Amenhotep and Simut. He took full responsibility for the death of his brother and begged that he and he alone of all the family should now be called to account.

All through this impassioned statement, the Prince had looked on with a non-committal air, certainly without the stern demeanour which might have been expected of him in such circumstances. When Siamun's voice faded and his head slumped forward in defeat, Khaemwase said, 'Sunero, look at his foot.'

This startled both Siamun and the Spy, the former because it was such an irrelevant remark, and the latter because it showed that the Prince had taken very careful note of every detail of the case. He could only have gained this knowledge from Harmose since neither Sunero nor Hatiay had mentioned the scarred footprints in any report. At a simple request, Siamun slipped off his sandal. There, across the heel of his foot, was a long, straight scar. Sunero sighed. There was no hope now.

Then, the Prince called in Takhepa who had been waiting in a side chamber but who had heard everything. She at once threw herself at the Prince's feet and renewed her plea for clemency. Siamun, already stunned at Takhepa's appearance, was even more amazed by what she was saying. She loved him! It was plain for all to see and hear. She loved him! At the end of all things, he had found love, and now that love would be denied him by the death sentence he knew he deserved.

Khaemwase held up his hand for silence. What he said then surprised everyone present. 'Enough! I have heard all your sorry tales. The whole business has gone on far too long and it bores me. I am almost minded to hand all the details over to the mayors of Waset and be done with it. Let them fight over jurisdiction. But it has produced its amusing moments as well as its annoyances. It has been instrumental in providing me with a highly effective group of officials, both for my own estates here in Waset and on the wider, national scene. I would not be boasting if I said that my servants are the best informed and the most dedicated in Kemet. I have already incurred the envy of certain people who would wish to lure those servants from me.'

This revelation was a surprise to everyone. In later discussions, no one admitted to having been approached with a better offer of employment which, since Khaemwase was already as close to the top of the pyramid of Kemet's society as anyone could get, would have had to come from another of his brothers, or even from the King himself. The Prince looked around at the assembly of Spy, Scribe and Harlot. 'I have been very lucky in finding such people and luckier still to have kept their loyalty. You,' and here he spoke directly to the Thief, 'are the reason why these people are here with me now. It is in order to catch you that they came together and have worked so successfully for all this time. In that regard, I have to thank you.'

There was a collective gasp. The Prince continued, 'I cannot, however, condone your thieving, no matter how justified you, or your father, or his father, thought you might have been. You have caused a great deal of upset for a large number of people, not least myself. You were the direct cause of a disagreement between myself and His Majesty, and no one can afford to disagree with the King. That disagreement led to your unfortunate brother falling foul of a trap set by a petty-minded official. So, you are and always will be responsible for your brother's death, but perhaps that knowledge is punishment enough.'

The Prince let his last few words settle in the ears of his astonished audience before he continued, 'The King is content that the thief – and you should note that His Majesty assumes only one thief – has met his just reward. As long as there is no further attempt on the Treasury, then no further suspicions will be aroused. This matter is closed. Hatiay, Sunero, leave us. I have things to discuss with this young couple.'

*

The Count and his wife found that they were clasping each other's hands and holding their breath almost as tightly. There was a shout from the lookout at the ship's bow. He pointed out the Temple of the King's father, the God Sethy, the colours of the painted reliefs on its walls already faded and mellowed with the years. A short distance ahead the King's Mansion temple loomed over the northern outskirts of the Western Town, while on the opposite bank of the river the pylons of the great Temple of Ipet Esut dominated the Eastern side of the City. They had arrived at Waset.

'Do we need to go over what I said to you and Takhepa?' the Prince asked.

The Count shook his head, 'I think we all know that, Sir. I went into that room expecting to hear sentence of death passed on me and yet I came out of it alive. I went in a humble stonemason and came out as a Designer on Your Highness' personal staff. I went in a simple citizen and came out with the title of Count.'

Takhepa interrupted him, 'You went in a single man and you came out betrothed to be married.'

'And you, my faithful Spy, did you feel betrayed, or defeated, or humiliated? Tell me now, before we reach the very end, what were your feelings when you knew that I had pardoned him for his audacity?'

'I was relieved, Sir. At last it was over. I could face Baketamen again with nothing to hide. I didn't have to be the bearer of more tragic news. The family, my family as I had come to see it, had been saved further misery. It was over.'

'And we all moved back to Mennefer and lived happily ever after, eh?' Khaemwase smiled weakly. 'Go, all of you. We shall be docking soon and after the midday meal, you, Count, will go and make your preparations to show us the last fragment of this story so that I can die content.'

Khaemwase had mentioned death. The Spy had clung to the faint hope that the voyage had worked a kind of magic and had wrought in his master that change of heart which the Count had so confidently predicted, but his former pessimism had now returned. The Prince had come to Waset to die.

The boat docked to considerable commotion on shore as the Prince's vessel was recognised only at the last moment and a proper reception committee had been hastily summoned, all the dignitaries having to be roused from their after-meal rest. They need not have bothered. Khaemwase stayed on board, simply sending out impersonal messages of thanks for the welcome. The Count went to arrange for their clandestine visit to the Mansion which would be the culmination of his plan and, if Sunero was right, the final act in the Prince's life.

Shortly before dawn the next day, a small party left the shadowy bulk of the Prince's barge to form a torchlit procession through the dockside lanes to the courtyard where donkeys were waiting. Takhepa complained of the indignity enforced on Khaemwase but the Prince waved aside her objection. The journey through the western suburbs and along the causeway to the Mansion was completed in almost total silence. They reached the massive gateway just as the sun had cleared the horizon behind them. The gigantic figure of the King slaying His enemies, carved in relief and brilliantly coloured, glowed in golden splendour from the pylons. The pennants on the flagpoles were beginning to flutter in the morning breeze and from beyond the bronze-clad gates could be heard the distant chanting of the morning ritual. There were no sentries at the ceremonial entrance. The doors were firmly bolted from the inside, but each of the lesser doors and the entrance to the adjacent northern temple were guarded by doorkeepers. Sunero had often wondered how the brothers had managed to evade the many guardians and temple servants to gain entry into the temple precincts.

The Count dismounted from his donkey and signalled for the rest of the party to do the same, then he instructed the donkey-handlers to take the beasts away. They were to wait in the Mansion's stable yard and the men would find food and drink with the temple stockmen. The Prince's personal attendant was more reluctant to leave his master but, eventually, the four principal players in the drama were alone.

'I am intrigued to see how we may progress from here,' said the Prince. 'Lead on, my dear Count.'

Without a word, Siamun indicated that Sunero should accompany the Prince while he took his wife's hand to lead the party around the northern end of the great pylon. A small, insignificant wooden gate was set in the end of the wall and, behind it, a steep stairway climbed high into the thickness of the pylon itself. Little light penetrated this narrow passageway at the best of times. At that early hour its deathly dark was punctuated only by the faint squares cast on the inner wall of the stairwell by the dawn light shining through small window openings. By the time the sun was at its height, even this meagre illumination would have disappeared. A patch of ever lightening sky was just visible at the top of the flight of steps but at the bottom only the first two deep treads could be picked out in the gloom.

'We go this way?' said the surprised Prince. As far as he knew, the stair gave access only to the top of the gateway. It was used by servants who changed or fixed the banners to the flagpoles. Takhepa looked worried. Although the day was young and the heat was not yet excessive, the steep climb in such a dark and confined space would be taxing, but she knew better than to suggest that Khaemwase should not attempt it. There was no going back now.

The gate was unlocked and there was no guardian. The Count opened it and set his foot on the first step. Takhepa followed, the Prince came behind her, and Sunero brought up the rear. There was barely enough space to move without rubbing shoulders against one wall or the other. The stair was more like a stone ladder best negotiated by feeling from one step to the next with both hands and feet. Takhepa hitched up her skirts to avoid treading or kneeling on the fabric. The Prince had to do the same with his heavy over-gown, worn against the morning chill. Sunero was grateful for the darkness which hid his master's indignity. Coming down, Sunero thought, it would be best and safest to go backwards.

At the top of the stairwell they had to duck into a low corridor which passed behind the flagpole niches. The golden dawn light shone through the row of windows which allowed access to the flag staves for attaching pennants. At the end of the narrow passage another short flight of steps led up to the roof of the pylon.

Siamun stumbled up the last few stairs to emerge, blinking, into the new dawn and turned to help his wife complete the climb. Khaemwase's breathing was laboured as he accepted Takhepa's outstretched arm to help him on to the roof. Sunero clambered out behind his master. Even the Spy felt rather weak at the knees. The parapet around the pylon was only knee- high, too low to lean upon. Instinctively they all kept to the middle of the roof. The Prince leaned forward, his hands on his thighs, gulping air into his tortured lungs. The Count's wife looked very worried but tried to hide her concern with inconsequential conversation.

'What a marvellous view from here. I could almost believe I was looking out from the walls of Hattusas.'

Sunero, realising that she was giving the Prince time to recover, said, 'With a stretch of the imagination, I suppose.' He was the only person present who could understand what the Hittite woman meant. The Hittite capital city was built on a high place with walls which seemed to grow from the very rock. The royal palace, built against the surrounding wall, had windows looking out over the foothills and down to the plain. The flatness of the Egyptian landscape could not be compared with such rugged grandeur and yet, Sunero felt he had to defend his homeland. 'The scenery is hardly the same, though, and it doesn't rain.'

'The occasional shower of rain would be refreshing. Perhaps you should adopt the Hittite weather god,' Takhepa said with a grateful smile at Sunero for taking up this line of conversation. 'Your land is so flat, your hills so puny. It is only the height and the effect of looking out over the valley that brings Hattusas to mind for certainly there are no other similarities. Even after all this time, I think I must be a little homesick. I had not realised how much I miss my own country.'

Sunero felt a catch at his heart. Another woman, in another place, at another time had said much the same to him. He had had no comfort to offer her then and had felt a pain that was almost physical as he acknowledged his helplessness. Takhepa was of stronger stuff. She had become a woman of Kemet in all things once she had married Siamun. Only the slight lisp in her pronunciation belied her foreign origins.

Siamun asked quietly, 'Are we ready to go on?'

The others looked to the Prince who nodded. The Count indicated the western side of the pylon, 'We're going over there.' At their raised eyebrows, he grinned and led them to the edge of the wall where the northern colonnade of the first court butted up against the pylon. He showed them a short wooden ladder which led down from the pylon to the roof of the colonnade and pointed out a similar ladder at the other end of the colonnade which gave access to the top of the second, smaller pylon.

'For the maintenance men,' he whispered. 'From here on we'll have to be quiet. The morning ritual will be over soon and there may be people moving about in this court and the next. They wouldn't normally look up here but it's best not to draw attention unnecessarily.' He took the lead down the ladder. Takhepa followed having again tucked up her skirts above her knees. The Prince, still unspeaking, followed with Sunero, as usual, at the rear.

Along the colonnade roof they went, as easily as walking across a stone pavement. Halfway along, Sunero felt the hairs on his neck rise as if someone was watching him, but there was not a living soul in the courtyard below. He paused to scan the area and discovered the source of his unease, so huge that at first he had not accepted its reality; the gigantic statue of the King himself, set to the left of the gateway into the second court. The sightless stone eyes, illuminated by the bright dawn, seemed to be staring straight at him. 'He is everywhere,' he thought, 'He knows his son is dying and he knows what we are doing.' Sunero shuddered at these irrational thoughts.

They went up the second ladder, taking them briefly on to the roof of the gateway, before descending another wooden stair on to the broader roof of the next colonnade. They moved stealthily, half crouching as the strains of the morning hymns issuing from the sanctuary became louder. At the western end of the colonnade, Siamun directed them across the court, passing over the entrance to the hypostyle hall. Once they had dropped down on to the roof of the hall, they were out of sight of anyone within the temple. The ceiling of the central aisle of the columned hall was higher than that to either side, allowing window grilles to be inserted between the massive pillars to admit light and air. Siamun indicated that they should not only keep silent but also stay far enough away from these grilles so that the flickering shadows of their passing should not draw the attention of the acolytes below.

At the far end of the hall there was another short drop to the roof of the western suite, a group of lesser halls and shrines and, as Sunero recognised with a lump in his throat, the Treasury. He knew they were now walking on the roof of the first and largest chamber where all the furniture was stored. He could picture the ghost of Harmose pacing up and down before the locked doors, oblivious of their approach to his realm, right over his head. A glance to his left showed him the masons' yard where work was just beginning. If someone down there should think to look up...

He tapped the Count on the shoulder and pointed. 'We're a bit exposed, don't you think?' he whispered.

'I've never done this in daylight,' Siamun admitted. 'I forgot how many people there would be around already at this time of day.' He looked unsure of himself, almost frightened. His face was pale beneath its usual tan.

Khaemwase spoke for the first time, 'We are on a spot tour of inspection,' he said in a droll tone, 'An official visit, authorised by me.'

'Even me?' Takhepa asked.

Siamun snorted and said, 'It's not far now, anyway,' and he led them on. His advance was, however, slow, even hesitant, his shoulders were stooped and his eyes fixed on the stone slabs beneath his feet. As he reached the next change in roof level, he stopped and took a long shuddering breath, 'We're here.' He eased himself down the drop of less than two cubits and sank to a sitting position with his back against the wall. He seemed to have forgotten about his wife and the others. Takhepa sat on the edge of the wall and demurely slid down before turning to offer a guiding hand to the Prince. Sunero joined them and they stood gazing down at the Count who had his head in his hands and was weeping quietly. Takhepa sat beside him and, without a word, put her arm about his shoulders.

Sunero was surprised by the suddenness of his friend's display of emotion, then he saw what Siamun had seen. At the point where the Count had stopped so abruptly, there were dark brown stains on several of the honey-coloured stones making up the wall and the roof. At first the Spy's eye dismissed them as natural variations in the colour of the sandstone from which they had been hewn, then he looked again and recognised the starred patterns formed by drops of dark liquid falling on to the stone. Next, he picked out a smear, almost like the trail of a careless paintbrush, up the wall beside Siamun's head. The most shocking discovery, despite being somewhat faded after all these years, was the handprint. Hari's blood. Of course, it had been dark when Siamun had left his brother's body in the Treasury below. He had not noticed how badly blood-stained his hands were, nor how blood was dripping through the basket that contained his brother's head. Now the full horror of what he had done had returned and he was reliving the whole grisly experience.

The Prince, embarrassed at the Count's unexpected mood swing, turned to study their surroundings, but he either failed to notice or tactfully ignored the bloodstains. He squatted on the roof and ran his hands over the joint between two massive stone slabs. He picked up a shred of twisted palm fibre, the remains of a rope. 'Where are we?' he asked Sunero.

'I would guess we're above the doorways to the innermost chambers of the Treasury, the precious goods stores. This wall,' he indicated the vertical they had just descended, 'must be the partition between the jar store and the last two rooms.' He paced out the width of the Treasury and confirmed his estimate. 'Yes, we're about over the doorway into the 'box and basket room' as Harmose called it.'

Siamun was still beyond speech. Khaemwase turned his attention back to the stone of the roof. 'What do you make of this, Sunero?' he said, pointing to a fine crack which meandered diagonally across one of the roofing slabs. 'And that?' he indicated the corner of another slab which was slightly tilted to be proud of the surrounding surface while its opposite corner was somewhat depressed.

'Bad workmanship, possibly,' Sunero suggested, knowing this not to be true.

Siamun spoke, 'There was nothing wrong with the craftsmanship. It was perfect when it was built but there have been some earth tremors in recent years and the ground on this side of the Mansion has shifted slightly. There are other places where stones have moved or twisted like this. Even the great statue of the King has developed cracks.'

Khaemwase looked interested, 'That is something I had not realised. I heard reports of the earth tremors, of course, but I had always imagined the Mansion to be unshakeable. Is it in any danger of collapsing?'

'No immediate danger,' Siamun sighed, 'It will outlast the King, have no fear of that, and probably his successors to the tenth generation, but it won't last for the millions of years the King expects. Every new tremor will weaken the structure and a really strong one could cause serious damage.' He shook himself and stood up, 'Let's see what we came to see.' He turned and placed his hands flat against the wall where he had been leaning. 'Give a hand, Sunero,' he said, as he began to push at the stone slab. The Spy suddenly understood what the old Architect Ahmose had done. One of the stones in the wall immediately above the doorway into the southern chamber was pivoted vertically about its centre line. It could be pushed in to create an entrance through which the would-be thief could drop into the innermost reaches of the Treasury itself. With a rope to facilitate his exit and the extraction of his spoils, the stone needed only to be pushed at its other end to close and perfectly disguise the entrance.

Khaemwase, too, had quickly grasped what Siamun was showing them and he beat Sunero to the wall to help the Count push the door open. Takhepa tried to stop him, resorting to an old familiarity in her anxiety, 'No, Khay, you must not. You are not strong enough. Sunero, help him!'

Siamun was now straining with his shoulder against the stone. Sunero overcame all caution and unceremoniously pushed his master aside to take his place beside the Count. Together they pushed and the stone began to move with a low, grinding rumble. Then it jammed. The two men pushed until both were sweating with exertion, but the stone would move no further. Sunero was the first to admit defeat. 'It's no good, Siamun, it's stuck. There's no moving it.' The gap they had created by pushing was hardly a palm's width.

'It must move, it must! I closed it by myself the last time. With two of us it should be easy. Now we pull.' Siamun moved to the opposite edge of the pivoting stone but even with Sunero's added muscle power and pulling with all their might they could not widen the opening. Siamun slumped over sobbing with frustration.

Khaemwase broke the disappointed silence. 'You said it yourself. This side of the temple has suffered from earthquake damage. The stone has been displaced enough to ruin the balance of the pivot. No one could open it now. I have seen enough. I know what I have puzzled over all these years. Ahmose was an ingenious man but his Secret has outlived its usefulness. The gods have had the last word. Come, suddenly I feel hungry. We shall go and beg breakfast at the Residence.'

To Sunero's amazement, the Prince pulled the unprotesting Siamun to his feet then offered Takhepa his help in renegotiating the wall. This was a different man from the stooping, enfeebled figure who had so recently staggered out at the top of the pylon stair. Khaemwase easily pulled himself up on to the roof of the hypostyle hall after

Takhepa, and arm in arm, the two retraced their steps, boldly striding out as if not caring who might see them. Sunero caught Siamun's arm and nodded towards the stone block protruding from the wall. With a deep sigh the Thief once again put his shoulder to the stone and by combining his strength with the Spy's managed to push it back in place. The result was less than perfect but Sunero was happy that the gap was now closed enough for no tell-tale crack of light to reveal the secret entrance to anyone in the Treasury below. Finally he bullied the Count into following Takhepa and the Prince and was further astonished that they were all able to reach the stairway without being spotted by any of the temple personnel who now thronged the surrounding administrative courts. Only when he was sitting in the reception hall of the Mansion Residence, supping superior wine from a fine glazed cup, did the enormity of their exploit finally strike him.

Chapter Twelve – Endgame

If the servants of the Residence were taken unawares by the appearance of the Crown Prince, they concealed their surprise well. Khaemwase was now lounging on the cushion-strewn divan, chatting cheerfully with Takhepa, recalling shared experiences and causing Siamun to sink ever further into a black depression. The Spy could find no words of comfort for his friend. The long agony of living with his brother's death on his conscience had been renewed with brutal suddenness. What should have been a final exorcism of that most dreadful of memories had, instead, become an overwhelming, painful experience. They had hoped to free the Prince from his melancholic state and in that they seemed to have succeeded, at least for the time being, but at what cost? Sunero found he could not imagine what would happen now. Everything had come to an abrupt halt. There was no future, no tomorrow.

There was a commotion in the outer hall. The Prince's body servant ran into the room, barely pausing to give the most cursory of bows to his master before muttering something to him in a low, anxious tone. Khaemwase sat bolt upright with a surprised frown on his face, and waved the man away.

'My friends, I must ask you to leave. It seems I have a visitor.'

The urgency in the Prince's voice made even Siamun pay attention. Takhepa leaned over to place a sisterly kiss on Khaemwase's brow before joining her husband. Then she turned, and with a tone of finality she said, 'Goodbye, My Lord.'

Sunero felt a shudder of apprehension run through him as he bowed and followed his friends from the room. In the antechamber, servants and guards were milling around like ants whose nest has been disturbed, but like ants, their actions had one basic plan and the Spy, the Count and the Hittite woman were caught up in the general upheaval. The major-domo flatly refused to let them out and they had to stand in line with the rest of the Mansion's servants. Clearly, the visitor's arrival was imminent and the degree of panic this had engendered pointed to his being only one person. As the doors were pulled open, the guards came to attention, the servants bowed low and the major-domo stepped forward to greet the King.

The bewildered official was pushed aside as His Majesty strode through the antechamber as unstoppable and single-minded as a charging bull. The doors of the audience hall closed behind him.

'How in Seth's name did he get here so fast?' the Count muttered.

'We did it,' Sunero reminded him, 'and he has far greater resources at his command than even the Prince. He is the King after all. Nothing escapes His Majesty's notice. The ripples caused by your arrangements must have reached the Palace almost before you told the Prince. What is truly amazing is that His Majesty should have bothered, dropped everything to chase after his son. What does he expect? What does he want? What does he know?'

Takhepa spoke quietly, 'He has come to take Khaemwase home.'

'Yes, but...' Sunero's voice trailed off as he saw the tears welling in Takhepa's eyes. She nodded. With a deep sigh he took Siamun's arm, 'Come along, my friend, we're no longer needed here.'

The Count looked from his wife to his friend. 'What now?' he said, 'What have I missed?'

'The King has arrived too late.'

'You can't mean... I don't believe it. We just left him. He was alive, laughing, happy. We won,' Siamun said, bewildered.

'There never was a contest, Siamun,' the Spy said with a sigh of resignation. 'We tried to tell you, the Prince told you. He came here to die and no one ever stood a chance of changing his mind. The King's arrival makes no difference. He may even have hastened the end.'

'No,' Takhepa said softly, 'He'll not die in his father's presence. He will be as astonished as we are that the King should have made this journey. Neither of them finds it easy to show his feelings, but by chasing after his son in this manner the King has shown more love for Khaemwase than ever before. Let them savour the last moments. Let them discover the truth of their love.'

Siamun was speechless. Sunero could only nod in agreement with Takhepa's words. He could not have expressed his own feelings as eloquently. The three remained standing in the antechamber waiting, though none of them knew what they were waiting for, only that they must wait.

It was past midday before the King left the building in another flurry of activity. As His Majesty swept past the bowing servants he caught Sunero's eye and a tiny frown flickered across his brow. The Spy knew that the summons would not be long in coming.

*

Khaemwase had faced his last interview with his father strengthened by an inner calm which came from knowing everything he had ever wanted to know. The King, with surprising restraint and in an uncharacteristically quiet voice, attempted to reason with his son, trying to renew his interest in life. The Crown Prince was not to be moved. There was nothing new to discover, no experience that he had not already savoured, no fight worth fighting, no reward worth winning. He could now admit to the illness which he had suffered for the last few months, the illness which he had refused to recognise and which he had kept at bay by sheer force of will. Now the final mystery was solved and his life was complete. Death was the next adventure and he was eager to embark on that journey of discovery.

The King had been shocked to see his son fading almost before his gaze. Despite His Majesty's divinity he knew he was powerless to halt the decline that Khaemwase seemed to have wished upon himself. Accepting the inevitable, the King gave his son his royal blessing, and then added the most human sentiment that Khaemwase had ever heard from him, 'Tell your mother I love her and that we'll all meet again soon.'

*

When the King summoned his own physician to attend the Prince, the friends knew beyond doubt that Takhepa was right. Finding that they were not needed, they slipped away to the familiar confines of the Mansion's scribal department. There, by physical eviction of the current occupant, they took possession of the office which Sunero had used for his discussions with Harmose during the Treasury investigations. There they found little to say, their hearts were so full, their thoughts so confused.

The Count shook his head in bewilderment and muttered, 'I never really thought he'd do it. I didn't think it was possible.' Takhepa patted his hand and murmured something soothing.

Sunero's common sense was arguing with his emotions as he tried to shoulder the blame for his master's demise. He was suddenly over-whelmed by the implications of that death. Despite having contemplated the possibility for many months, now that the event was close at hand, he could not envisage a future without the Prince. He realised, with a physical jolt of emotion, that over the last desperate month his respect for Khaemwase had turned into something greater, something deeper. He glanced up to find Takhepa looking at him and he was lost. Without a word being spoken she gathered the two men in her arms and together they wept.

The messenger who knocked at the office door hesitated only a moment before opening it, giving the friends no time to compose themselves. The young man was either oblivious to their grief or tactfully ignored it. 'At last, I've found you. No one seemed to know where you might be, this was almost my last hope.'

Sunero unselfconsciously wiped his eyes and studied the newcomer. There was something familiar about him, something about the mouth. 'Hatiay?' he said, knowing at once that this was impossible.

'Khay, son of Hatiay,' the messenger smiled. Takhepa sniffed back a tear at the mention of the Prince's familiar name.

The young man continued, 'People have been sent all over the place looking for you.'

'What have we done now?' Siamun asked.

'Nothing that I'm aware of,' Khay said, 'but the King wants to see you.'

'The King?' they said in unison.

'Yes, so I suggest you don't keep His Majesty waiting any longer than necessary.'

*

They entered the Royal Presence with mixed feelings, not knowing what to expect. Siamun was particularly worried as he had no idea how much Khaemwase had told the King about his involvement in the Treasury thefts. He sensed the death sentence, suspended all those years ago, now descending upon him. He held Takhepa's hand tightly in his own as if frightened that, once letting go, he would never hold it again. Sunero felt surprisingly calm at the prospect of this interview. His long association with the Royal Family had hardened him to their ways and their words. There was nothing that the King could do or say that would perturb him in the slightest. Although life without Khaemwase would be less colourful, less challenging, less interesting, life would go on. The King would go on and they were all the King's subjects, to do with as His Majesty pleased.

The audiences were brief and to the point, much as they had come to expect of the King. He spoke to each in turn, in private.

Despite the subdued atmosphere of the Mansion Residence, with servants creeping around, fearful of making a noise, and most of the daily administrative affairs having been set to one side, the King was business-like and economical with his words. Some of these words were meant to remain private, others were to be considered over the coming days and responses prepared. When they left His Majesty's audience chamber, the three friends had much to think about.

*

The end came swiftly. Khaemwase slipped into a sleep from which he would not wake and passed away with the sunset on the day following the revelation of the Secret. In later days, people of the Holy City would claim that dogs howled and lamps flickered at the very moment that the Prince's spirit left his body. Such folk tales have always arisen around characters of great personality or great power, and Khaemwase was both. Sunero hoped that his master would know how much the people of Waset had appreciated him even if it had taken his death for them to realise it. A period of official mourning was proclaimed in Waset while the embalmers prepared the Prince's body for the tomb. To everyone's surprise, the King Himself remained in the Holy City for the full seventy days and showed genuine emotion when making offerings to the Crown Prince's memory in the Mansion Temple. Khaemwase would be remembered there forever, finally fulfilling his prophetic name, 'Glory in Waset'.

The funeral voyage back to Mennefer was a prolonged affair. The boats stopped at every town along the route where there was a temple or major shrine to Ptah, the Prince's personal patron. At every halt more mourners joined the party so that a large flotilla assembled to escort Khaemwase to his last resting place. The vault in the Apis gallery tomb, though slightly larger, was less regal in its decoration than the chambers prepared for his royal brothers in the Great Place, and he had only his beloved bulls for company, but everyone, even the King, knew that this was what Khaemwase wanted. The Prince's eldest son found his position as director of the funerary ritual usurped as the King himself insisted on performing the Opening of the Mouth ceremony to restore the powers of speech, sight and hearing for the deceased. While the family mourned, thinking their private and very different thoughts about Khaemwase, many ordinary people, whose lives he had touched in one way or another, paid their personal tributes to the Prince by making offerings at the local shrines to Ptah. Sunero and Siamun chose to pay their respects at the Apis sanctuary.

'You can see how the beast has grown since we were last here,' Siamun said, waving a handful of freshly plucked grass to tempt the young bull over to them where they leaned on the enclosure fence. Sunero nodded. The animal had filled out and was looking sleek with a hide that shone with health as he trotted over to meet his friends.

'He still behaves like a calf,' the Spy said as he scratched the bull's nose, 'He hasn't quite grown into his dignity.'

'A few heifers will soon change that,' Siamun said with a wink. 'Have you ever thought, Sunero, that the Prince's spirit might be drawn to this place. He was so involved with the Apis I can't imagine he would want to lose contact with this chap.' He tipped his head as if listening for the bull to speak. Sunero was surprised at this line of thought from his otherwise down-to-earth friend, but he had to admit that the same idea had occurred to him, usually on dark nights when sleep would not come.

He looked at Siamun's face, deeply tanned and lined with creases of age. He studied the shiny bald patch and the receding hairline. He noted the glistening tears in the corners of those slate-grey eyes. He put a hand on the Count's shoulder, 'You loved him too, didn't you?'

Siamun smiled, an easy smile, 'I suppose I must have done.'

'So, having admitted that at last, where do we go from here?'

'Have you made your decision yet?'

'What decision was there to make? When the King offers you a position in the Royal Household it's hardly sensible to turn it down. Anyway, I'd be lost without something to do. I may be getting old but I'm not yet ready to retire, and what else do I know?'

'So what title is His Majesty bestowing on you?'

'None. Apparently I'm already a Count by right of property – I'll tell you all about it some time – but that sort of thing can sometimes be a hindrance in my line of work so I'll only use it when there's a need to impress.'

'So our titles match, eh? We're equal in status after all. Baketi would have loved that,' but seeing Sunero's frown, the Count instantly regretted mentioning his sister. To cover his embarrassment he said, quickly, 'So, what do we call you now?'

'What do you mean? I'm still Sunero.'

'Of course you are, but to me, to Takhepa, to everyone, you'll always be the Prince's Spy.'

Sunero said, with a pale smile, 'Once I would have resented that but now...now I think that's as good a way to be remembered as any.'

Printed in Great Britain
by Amazon

32929584R00096